Deep Pink

SARAH A. HOYT

GOLDPORT PRESS

1 TO THE PINK!

MANY PEOPLE HAVE TOLD ME TO GO TO HELL. Happens to all PIs, I guess. And being a PI named Seamus — Seamus Magis, at your service — it was inevitable.

But I never thought I'd have to go. Certainly not for a case.

How it started was like this: My friend Rod Rando was the manager for a lot of metal bands. Well known properties, like Goat Eternity and Bestial Cadaver and Edge of Skulls.

He'd done great out of it. Like, he'd married a bunch of mOdells, one after the other, and his alimony bills were epic, but with all that he still had his offices in the penthouse of this steel and glass high rise downtown, a place so clean you could lick the floor and probably emerge in better health and so classy that if you put Marx inside it, he'd have melted to a little puddle of goo on the floor.

Honest, I felt out of place just going in, in my jeans and T-shirt.

Oh, sure, Rando also wore jeans and T-shirts, but his were designer, carefully torn and scuffed. I mean, someone had made six figures just figuring out where to rip that denim, or where to put the stain on his shirt so it looked like someone had stepped on it.

He'd called me in because starting about two years ago he'd noticed some of his bands, the ones who had been the most serious about their satanic symbols and altars and rituals and what not ... changing style.

Look, it wasn't so much that they changed, though sure, that would be bad enough. When you're administering a multi-million dollar talent, you get a little scared by change. Who knows if the fans will like it?

And this change was really weird. Suddenly these supposedly dark, satanic artists were wearing all pink, their music sounded disturbingly like K-Pop, and instead of the horns, they made heart signs with their hands. And one of them, the Filthy Blood Whores had changed their name to Pink Fluffy

1

Kittens and wore pink cat ear headbands.

Their fans had no idea what to make of it, but my friend did. "Someone is giving them drugs," he said. "And it must be some good shit, because it's spreading from band to band.

"I mean, when Satan's Handmaidens sang Pretty Pink Bubbles at their concert, the fans stormed the stage in fury and put them in the hospital. It's that bad. But they didn't change back. And it keeps spreading. Even though the new style bands are tanking, others keep changing to imitate them. And then they also don't sell for shit. I can't afford this."

He raked his hand backward across his unkempt, thinning but long hair. It was like the less hair he had on top, the more he let it grow, till now the stringy ends brushed the middle of his back.

"Leb, I need help."

Sigh. Okay, okay. So my name is Seamus Lebanon Magis. Are you happy? Stop laughing. I was named after my mom. I should just be grateful they hadn't given me her full name: Cedar of Lebanon Magis. Rod is one of the few people who even knows my full name, and... other things, so of course I said, "I'll help if I can. I just don't see what I can do."

"It has to be drugs."

"You mean they weren't on drugs before?" I asked. If I sounded skeptical, it was because I'd heard some of their acts.

"Oh, hell no. I don't mean that. I mean, actually mostly they prefer alcohol, but sometimes, you know, some uppers, some downers, some ayahuasca... Thing is, I get those drugs first, then pass them on to the guys, after making sure they're clean. I monitor the alcohol they get, too. I make sure it's nothing that will fry their brains."

"I didn't just hear that."

"Whatever. You can't let your bread and butter go to seed. But this shit ... whatever it is ... this is some crazy shit. I mean, hell, I didn't even know Choke Slave could sing falsetto." He dropped onto his custom made ergonomic chair and put his feet on his blue glass desk big enough and probably sturdy enough to park a Mack truck on. "I want you to find the people responsible and stop this shit."

That was obviously my cue.

Which is how I found myself in the apartment of one Albert Schneider, aka Thrall of Darkness, aka Pink Plush Sorbet, on a hungover Saturday morning.

Okay, so, just so you get the problem, his apartment looked like a Disney princess had exploded all over it. Nah, make that a set of Disney princesses. There had to have been a lot of them for all that pink, glitter, frills and lace to have gone everywhere. Like, there was glitter on the ceiling.

And then there were stuffed animals. They were piled on the ratty sofas. They were stacked in the corners. They overflowed the window sills. There were all kinds, but most were kittens and puppies with big, round glass eyes. Some were tiny. Some were almost my size. And all looked the worse for the wear, as if he'd bought them used in thrift shops.

In a corner, a figure of Hello Kitty had pink scented candles lit in front of it. If it weren't for the sheer oddity, I'd think it was an altar.

Albert was on the wrong side of thirty, and I'd bet if he hadn't dyed his hair flat black, it would have been mostly white. He was long haired, with a chest-long braided beard, and incongruous fake glittery-pink eyelashes. There were pink beads on the beard, too. He wore a sort of pink jumpsuit thing, with a silver glitter belt, like some intergalactic federation was trying out uniforms that got in touch with its feminine side. For some reason it just made his mean, hard eyes look harder and meaner. He glared at me. "What the hell do you mean, am I gay?"

I looked around the apartment.

He made a suggestion that would require my breaking my spine, or possibly bilocating.

"Fuck, man," he added. "I'm just what I've always been. A servant of the dark."

"The dark ... pink?" I asked.

He shook his head. The glare was hard enough to cut but there was something else behind it, something stark and cold. Fear? "New management, man. New management."

"What do you mean new management? Do you mean Rod Rando? I thought–"

He looked at me as though I were too stupid to live. "Not Rando. Rando is ... nobody in this. Oh, sure," he waved it all away, "he's an okay agent, right? But this is The Management," he said. "Down below."

From somewhere – I'll swear – came the sound of tut-tut and "don't talk" uttered in a girlish voice, and Schneider shook and went pale. "I've already said too much, man. The new management is ruthless. They ain't got no sense of humor. None whatsoever."

I was about to tell him devils never had any humor, when it occurred to me this grown man wearing bright pink and lighting candles to Hello Kitty was dead serious. He really thought that something or someone would punish him for talking out of turn. Which meant he really had thought he was serving Satan or something. "Are you for real?" I asked. "Do you mean to tell me that Sat–"

"Peggy," he said. Fear flared behind his eyes like a defective neon. " sign. "Just call him Peggy."

His voice had a note of hysteria. I couldn't get him to make any more sense and was starting to warm to the "weird drug hypothesis."

But the next morning Albert Schneider, aka Thrall of Darkness, aka Pink Plush Sorbet, was found in his apartment with his throat cut and something carved on his forehead that looked suspiciously like cat ears.

And I had a voice mail from Rando.

2 A CALL FROM THE PAST

I'D BEEN OUT MOST OF THE NIGHT, going from club to club, to listen to some of the bands Rando managed.

Satanic Death Metal has never been my thing. I guess I never believed in God enough to really hold against Him everything that's fucked up in the world, much less to ally myself with the other side.

But I'd gone from club to club all over Cleveland, using a pass Rod gave me, trying to trace the spread of the infection.

"I don't even know what has caused the style change," Rando had said. "Or which bands have done it. They don't tell me, of course. Until I hear some of their fans have fucked them up, or someone calls me to ask me why Demonic Feast is now calling itself Sparkle Love Fun."

That's why I'd gone from club to club, and auditorium to auditorium, looking over some of Rando's clients, trying to figure out the scope of the infection.

So far in town, ten for ten of the bands I'd seen had gone to the pink. I had gotten a card with their original names from Rando, but now they were all wrong.

Polishing the Knob of Hell was now Light Delights, and its six surly members wore pink wigs and sang in constantly breaking falsetto.

Headless Vampire called itself Royal Bunny Hearts and– But what's the use? You get the idea.

I found that songs sung in a falsetto by people totally unsuited to that register gave me a splitting headache, and that their bewildered fans sweated even more profusely than your average crammed-together bar or club audience and got even more aggressive when confronted with what could be badly done K-pop.

I thought one of the fans of the former Satanic Monkeys, now Pretty Puppy Tails, was going to punch me in the face when I told him they looked funny in their pink heart necklaces. He probably thought so, he'd hit me too, but thankfully broke down crying before he punched me.

Anyway, the sound level had been so high in all those clubs that I hadn't actually heard my phone ringing in my pocket, and it wasn't till I took it out previous to falling on my face on the bed, I saw I had two voice mails.

The first was from Rando and he sounded as I felt, like he'd been dragged backwards through Hell, hitting all the spiky spots. "Bertie Schneider got himself killed, the dumb bastard," he said. "Are you any closer to figuring out why they're going crazy? Call me!"

I glared at the screen. I'd call him after I napped. Maybe. Right then I just wanted to tell him "Yeah, it's some weird drugs," and leave it at that. What did he expect me to do? Threaten these crazy people into singing obsessively about evil and Satan again? What would I threaten them with? I mean, when people throw their support and devotion to the master of darkness and evil, what are they afraid of, really?

Then I thought of Bertie Schneider and the look of terror in his eyes when he'd said, Just call him Peggy. And shuddered.

And with my luck Rod would want me to go and track down the supplier of the weird drugs. Which was not something I could do. Even if such a supplier existed. Not for something on this scale. It would take police.

The second voice mail was from a number I didn't recognize. I pushed play and heard a voice that took me right back to high school. "Leb?" a woman said, "I'm in trouble and I need your help. I thought … well, never mind. I heard you might be able to help, so … oh, never mind. The whole thing is so crazy. So sorry to bother you."

And had it been anyone else, I would have "never minded." The problem is I recognized the voice.

When it comes to women, Heavy Metal is less accurate than Country. At least Country gets it that some women come into your life for the purpose of messing it up and that you never get over them.

Emma Marie Accorso was one of those. Or at least she was that one, for me. I'd fallen head over heels for her the moment I met her, on the very first day of kindergarten, waiting to go into Mrs. Hooey's classroom.

Thirty years later, I still remembered as if it were yesterday: the little girl with her red hair in pigtails and the big green eyes, wearing the orange T-shirt and the scruffy jean shorts.

At recess I'd pulled her pigtails and made fun of her freckles, because that's what kindergarten love looks like. And she'd called me four eyes and kicked me in the shins. So I guess she'd liked me too.

We'd been friends ever since, elementary, middle school and high school. Lost touch with her in college, because she'd gone out of town, and I'd been heartbroken when I heard through mutual friends that she'd married a dentist. Not that I had any right to object, because – because our relationship had never been like that.

I'd never had the courage to tell her I loved her, and I guess she only wanted me as a friend.

She'd grown up from the little pigtails and the tomboy scruffiness to a lovely, slim young woman with eyes that looked too big for her face, but we'd stayed friends – just friends – friends who told each other everything, and sometimes took long, long walks around the neighborhood, and who were the only ones who could understand what the other read or listened to or liked. We'd stayed like that, like people hesitating at the edge of the ocean, wetting their feet but never going in, because it might be cold. And then I'd heard she'd got married.

And now she was calling me.

Yeah, Rod could wait. I looked at the number Emma had called from and called back. At the last minute, I realized anyone could answer, even her husband or her kid, and then what would I say? I almost hung up, but just then, I heard Emma. "Hello?" She sounded tired.

"Emma."

"Leb!" she said. Then stopped. "Oh, hell, Leb, I shouldn't have called you."

Humans are funny creatures. We don't reason from known facts. We don't, in fact, reason from unknown facts either. When our heart is involved, we don't reason at all. I leapt from that sentence, that tone of voice, and imagined her needing a detective to help research mitigating circumstances because she had stabbed the dentist through the heart with a sharpened toothbrush. In my mind, I saw her led away in shackles, and—

"What's wrong?" I asked, afraid my voice betrayed my fears. "What happened?"

"It's one of my children," she said. "She's missing."

Oh. That was a horrible thing, and I didn't know what to say, but why shouldn't she have called? "I find missing children," I said. Granted, not often. Most of the time what I did was more along the lines of finding who the father of the child really was. It's a dirty world out there, and my business just means I sometimes walk in all the crap up to my knees.

"Yes, but… Emma sniffled. "She's been missing for two weeks. It's just that her parents say I killed her and … and the police are going to dig up my backyard."

She sounded like she was about to cry and the whole thing made no sense. I focused on the weirdest part, "Her parents? I thought she was your daughter?"

There was an intake of breath, something that might have been suppressed laughter. "No. Lilly isn't my daughter. Oh, I see, because I said she was one of my children. They're not my children, exactly. I mean, I don't have any children of my own. But I'm at home all the time. It's not normal in the neighborhood. So a lot of the kids around here come to me after school. Because there's no one at their home. And I'm always here. Because of Mom."

"Mom? Your mom?" And then proving my wonderful deductive capabilities. "You're in town." Because, yeah, that was the really important part.

"Yeah. When I finished college, Mom was having … episodes. The doctor said it was early onset Alzheimer's, and I came back to look after her, only I can't– Never mind that. Lilly Michal Jones came here all the time after school. Her parents knew that. They didn't–" She paused, then said, in a rush as if the words were very important to get out in case I wanted to stop her or something. "They didn't care. But then she disappeared. She didn't disappear from here. I haven't seen her in two weeks, but they say I kidnapped her or killed her. The policehave been all over the house, and now they … they're digging up the yard. Today. Oh, Leb. I'm worried sick about her, and I don't know what happened, or why they're going after me."

"Okay," I said. Being hit at once with the idea that there had never been a dentist and that someone thought that Emma could have hurt a child, my brain short circuited, I went into automatic. "Okay. Not a problem. I'll come by, okay? Would this afternoon be okay?"

"Yeah," she said. "This afternoon. They'll probably be digging up my roses. I don't know what to do. It's going to upset Mom so much."

"I'll be by soon. I promise."

"Thank you, Leb. Thank you so much."

"I'll get there as soon as I can. It's just I haven't gone to bed– I haven't slept yet."

"Ah," she said. "I don't think there's any rush. She's been missing two weeks and the police–"

"I never know what I can do till I try. Don't worry, Emma, I'll be by." Which I supposed is what love looked like at thirty five, when you were a bottom-feeding PI living in a tiny apartment at the edge of the barely-safe area of town, surrounded by fourth hand furniture bought at garage sales. Look, you do what you can. I felt like my life had taken a wrong turn somewhere, sure, but how do you fix that? No one made turn-arounds for lives. "Give me your address?"

She did. While I talked on the phone, I caught a glimpse of myself in the mirror, black T-shirt stained and pulled askew, hair that really could use a cut. Maybe there were still eyes in the middle of the dark circles that took up most of my face. It was hard to tell. The dark circles were so big.

I looked like I'd been out all night, in dens of iniquity. Which in fact, I'd been, but for money. Of course that didn't sound good at all, now that I thought about it. I hung up on Emma with more reassurances, most of them probably lies and called Rod.

"About damn time," were the first words I heard, which tells you why I stop everything to work for Rod. It's that kind of confidence and warm friendship that compensates for all the weirdness and trouble. Okay, that and unlike most of my clients, he didn't skip out on the bill. It was followed by, "What have you found out?"

"That all ten of those bands have gone to the pink," I said.

He said something really rude about pink. Probably unwarranted. I mean, there was nothing actually wrong with pink as a color.

"You said Schneider died? How?" I asked, as I undressed. There is an art to undressing with a phone to your ear. I'd long since mastered it. In my business, client is just a term for people who aren't in a relationship with you, but pay you to hold their hands. Which also sounded totally wrong.

"Not died. Not died, man," Rod sounded like he hadn't slept even for a few minutes, either, like he'd spent the entire night in a grudge match with his worries. "Got himself killed."

"Yeah?" It seemed to me – and mind you I don't read industry news – that it was wasn't all that rare right? Drug dealers, and all that. Or perhaps a drug overdose. "How?" I grabbed clean clothes and laid them out on the bed. Then glared at the stains on the T-shirt and got a button down. It was no great shakes as a button down, starting to fray around the collar and cuffs, but I wanted to look halfway decent if I was going to see Emma. How stupid do you have to be for your heart to pound at the thought of seeing a girl you'd fallen in love with in kindergarten, a girl who only called you because she was in trouble? Don't answer that. I liked my illusions.

There was a hesitation, and I heard Rod swallowing. "Throat cut from ear to ear. It was bad, man. They called me because the dumb bastard had me listed on his forms as next of kin, because– Never mind. There was blood everywhere. You have to figure out what's going on."

"Are you sure it has anything to do with the case?" I remembered Albert Schneider's apartment. Let's say I hoped his band was more successful before he'd gone to the pink, because where he was living now was one step above the projects. If it was one step above. The kind of apartment complex where people hang out around at noon on a work day wearing pajamas or less. The kind of apartment complex that's haunted by large packs of feralized children, and where the lights in the parking lot are bright enough to allow you to perform brain surgery at midnight. And where the police do twice-hourly drive-bys. And where cars still get jacked, homes still get broken into, despite police presence. "It could have been a break in, or–"

Rod made a sound he probably thought was a laugh, but which sounded somewhere between a groan and a cough. "Someone…." He paused, and I had the distinct impression he was swallowing to avoid being sick. "Someone had left little cutesy paw-prints in his blood all over the carpet. Someone painted a heart on the wall and the words Don't talk. Kthanxbye."

I dropped to sitting on my bed. "He was killed by a lolcat?"

"It's not funny."

"No, I suppose not." Though as death went, it seemed to be hilarious, if in a really dark and demented way. Actually, the whole "pink thing" was funny in a really dark and demented way.

"Trust me, no one deserves to go that way. That apartment...."

"I hear you. I'll look around. I'm leaning toward the weird drug hypothesis."

"Did he tell you that he was taking something? Give you any clue?"

"No. It was more, you know, a feeling."

"Well, what did he tell you that caused someone to cut his throat?"

I took the question with me into the shower. Peggy? Could that be it?

Showering in ice cold water, shaving and putting on clean clothes, doesn't compensate for having spent the night awake. But if you drink enough coffee afterwards, it can sort of help. A bit. I mean, you're still half asleep, but now you are having what seem to be vivid dreams that are a lot like work.

While drinking the coffee, I opened my laptop and looked up Albert Schneider's death. There wasn't anything. I mean, all the hits were for his one hit song, Dead Pigs in Hell. Right. That wasn't going to do anything. There was an interview with him shortly after the song came out. Let's say he looked better dressed in black than in pink. At least the look of death warmed over made more sense.

The search for Lilly Michal Jones, on the other hand brought up article after article.

And I started to understand the size of Emma's problem.

Mr. and Mrs. Jones, or rather Corentin Jones & Signy Harrington, were a power couple, a marriage made in Ivy League law school and blessed with partnerships in the best firms in town, if not the state.

Looking at their pictures, at first glance it was hard not to think this wasn't a marriage between fraternal twins: they were not only both elegant and blond, but they both dressed in exquisitely cut suits (hers sometimes a skirt suit) and never seemed to have a hair out of place.

Yes, being on the short and squat end of human normal, with hair that stays in place for about two seconds after being combed – on a windless day – I tend to dislike such people on sight, and have tried to popularize a rumor that they're all produced in a factory in the depths of China. But I knew, of course, that what hurt me was envy.

I was never going to look like that. I was never going to be a success story. It would take days to describe what I'd never do or be. It was easier to say what I'd always be: a dead-end PI in a dying town.

Jones-Harrington had it all: the big house – featured in a magazine spread – the foreign vacations – shown on their social media – the looks, the glamour, the glitz, the high powered careers. What they didn't have was the

1.8 children. They had one child, Lilly. And no dog, I guessed because a dog would be too much work or impinge too much on their social life or perhaps shed all over their fashionably-dark apartment.

Okay, that was unkind, but it seemed to me that even in the articles about their daughter's disappearance, all they wanted to talk about was how important they were and how the search was taking time from their lives and somehow hampering their career. That the journalists wrote this down without realizing how self-absorbed these two sounded was amazing.

Lilly, shown in a few fuzzy pictures, reminded me of Emma as a child: a tomboy, all elbows and knees, with reddish pigtails and big green eyes. All her pictures were a little blurred, as though she were always in movement. They captured her in a playground, and squirming atop a wall, and grinning in what looked like the local school entrance.

As far as I could tell, Lilly had disappeared from her bedroom in their high priced home, on summer solstice night. Never to be heard from again.

The idea chilled me. I felt as sorry for the poor kid as I felt exasperated by her parents.

So, I'm a sap. Stories of missing children make me want to cry. It's not that I think they're all sweetness and light, okay? I know they aren't. I still remember being a vengeful, whiny conniving little kid myself.

But they don't know they're not sweetness and light and, more importantly, they've been taught to expect the best of adults and bystanders, particularly when they're spoiled, given-everything-from-birth little kids like Lilly Jones. They don't – yet – understand what the world is all about. They think that no matter what they do or say, they will be treated with kindness. A disruption of that pact is unfair, because they're not aware it can be disrupted. It smacks too much of betrayal.

Adults can be betrayed too, but we know betrayal is not only in the realm of possible, but frankly likely. Scarred skin cuts less easily, and so do scarred feelings. And the hurt doesn't come as a surprise.

I wondered where she was. I knew the statistics as well as anyone else, okay? After forty eight hours the chances of finding a little kid alive were next to none.

In the more recent articles Emma's name appeared. Her place honestly seemed to be the only regular haunt of the kid, outside school and home.

They described Emma as unemployed and the reporters managed to sneak in the idea that she was frustrated and perhaps jealous of the Harrington-Jones and therefore might have stolen or harmed their daughter.

I got up, shaking my head. Honestly, half the time what the police did was what any public service did: manage the situation and calm the public. They seemed to have absolutely no leads, but because the parents wouldn't shut up about Emma, and the parents were big fish, the police needed to look like they were doing something. Harassing Emma was doing something. Probably nothing productive, mind you, but something.

I closed my computer, and grabbed my coat. Yeah, sure, it was September, and the chances of my needing a coat were low during the day, but I had the button down shirt on, and with the dark sports coat, I looked semi-presentable, should presentability come into question, such as for instance spending some time arguing with the police to get them to not dig up Emma's roses, or maybe to dig them up gently.

My car is not exactly on its last legs. Technically it's past its last legs, and has been necromantically resurrected for the purpose of hauling me around. In fact, I was fresh out of necromantic powers, and just fixed things myself or took it to a buddy's garage, and had probably replaced the entire engine over time. It's older than me. It's a 1978 Chevy Suburban, with a missing front bumper and the front left side crunched in. It has a range of sounds like you wouldn't believe at the slightest movement. And it got – I swear – eight miles to the gallon, on a good day. It was, to an extent, responsible for my state of penury just because of how much it cost to drive anywhere. I've nicknamed it The Brown Disgrace.

I hadn't done it, honest. The dents, I mean.

What happened was that my practical little – old – Taurus had finally gone to the happy racing grounds the year before, at age 25, leaving me with a dead car and a just-received $800 fee in the bank.

I dare you to find a car for that price. At least one with four wheels that turn, and which will actually carry you places.

Turns out the owner of this Suburban had been in an accident a year before, bought something brand spanking new, and left this one sitting on the yard of his farm for a year, before kind of sort of deciding maybe he could put it up for sale.

I'd got it for $700 and it drove and everything, even if it looked like hell approaching you from behind.

Mind you, I'd had to clean the chicken feathers and crap, because while in the farm yard, it had housed fowl.

To be fair, I'd also found two eggs under the seats right after I bought the car, and they were still good. So, there's that. Unexpected bonus: a cheap dinner.

In the year I'd had it, I'd found its looks were an advantage. If you're pushing the speed limit, or turning a little too tight at intersections, a car that looks that banged up buys you a kind of immunity. Police won't pull you over, because they figure you're just going to skip out on the traffic ticket and not really care about points on your license. And other drivers when they see you approach instinctively think that not only are you a reckless driver, but you just don't care. I mean, if you cared you'd have the dents pulled out, right? And maybe have a bumper put back in.

So other cars skeedadle out of the way as fast as their wheels will carry them, the traffic cops avoid you, and you get where you were going that much faster. As long as where you were going wasn't a place with valet parking, because you get there faster too, but the valets give you the weirdest looks.

Another advantage of the Suburban was that if I had a really bad six months and lost my apartment, I could always live in the back. It was almost as big as Rod's desk.

For the first time I wondered what people would think of my car. People in this case being, of course, defined as Emma.

But there was nothing for it. It's not like I could change myself overnight, to be in the life I wanted to be. It would have started out at marrying Emma as soon as we finished high school, I thought. Which was silly. It wasn't like she would have married me if I'd only asked.

So I tried to put it out of my mind – does this work for other people? It's never worked for me – while I dialed up the number of a cop I know, set the phone on the seat next to me, and started up the car.

"Hey, Mike," I said, when he answered. "I'm looking into something related to Albert Schneider. I hear he was a suspicious death?"

3 UNFUNNY MURDER

MIKE, ANOTHER HIGH SCHOOL CLASSMATE – we used to play D & D together back in dear old Dinkhelsbuhl – said, "Are you investigating? Because if so, you're out of your depth. This is some deranged, ritualistic crap."

I wasn't sure whether to be insulted that he thought I couldn't investigate important cases, or relieved he thought I wouldn't be involved in deranged ritual murder cases. He should have seen some of the divorces I'd worked on. "No. Not investigating his death, if that's what you mean," though I remembered the tut tut and wondered at the message on the wall if it was true. "I'm looking into a problem with Rando's bands, and Schneider was in one of them. I don't think it's related. Probably. Except in the sense maybe one of his bandmates was involved."

I could almost hear Mike shaking his head over the phone. When you've been friends a long time, you kind of get "silent denial" without having to see it. "Nah," he said. "Nah. Not his band mates, man. They were performing at the Cat and Tails. In front of like 300 people, when it happened. They were pretty pissed Bertie hadn't shown up."

"I see. At any rate, if I come in…."

"Sure. It's not like I'm going to give you anything that won't hit the papers in a few hours, but sure, come on down."

I went on down.

Though because I'm not stupid, and because some stereotypes are true, I first stopped by the corner doughnut shop. You can keep your high priced caffeine and espresso shops. This place – Jill's Rounds – was a family store that had been there for at least two generations, and their jelly doughnuts were to die for. Which is why I got half a dozen of them and two of their mega-giganto – yeah, that's what they called them – cups of black coffee, which were advertised as large enough to drown in, and almost were.

The police station is a seventies building set in between two Victorians. Someone had demolished two or three Victorians to put in this low-slung, flat roofed building. At least they'd stopped painting it green, which it still had been ten years ago. It still looked pretty bad, and the roofs leaked, but at least it didn't scream "Taste came here to die" to aliens in low Earth orbit.

I went in through the front. At some point, it had been an open-style design – who thought that was a good idea with a police station? – and like almost all such buildings, it had got retrofitted for actual human use and away from "Architect's wet dream." In the large reception area, that mostly meant cubicle-partitions in scuffed-grey cloth-like material. This was where the secretarial, clerical and general record-keeping went on. Towards the back there were actual places where cops and suspects talked and suspects were booked or whatever, and those had been set off with real walls. The modifications made the whole building look like a maze for tortured rats who would never ever find any cheese. Which, now I think about it, was probably right.

In front of all the clerical cubicles – where you could hear the noise of a hundred conversations and fifty keyboards – was a grey metal desk with a computer on it. Behind the desk, on a foldable chair was Josh Russell. That is, Seargent Josh Russell, who mostly got tapped for intake, and hated it, but would lump it while he was a relative rookie.

Around the desk on the other side were about a dozen Detectives, each of them accompanying or leading a mixed mess of humanity. And trust me when I say "mess." Some of the people were in handcuffs, and one extremely thin young man, with a spaced out look on his face kept screaming they were coming for him. Whoever they were must have lived midair above Josh's head, because that's where he was staring, intently. Thoroughly methed up, was my guess.

"Hey, Josh," I said. "Here to see Mike. Detective Flores."

He waved at me, while typing with one hand. "His office."

Which was one way of indicating directions. Except for where this was the kind of labyrinth where the Minotaur would have starved to death trying to find anything, up to and including the Argonauts.

I took three wrong turns, and opened the door to what turned out to be a cleaning closet and one to some kind of conference room, where two guys sat at a table, and one guy stood at a white board. All of them looked at me in surprise, and I apologized and continued down the hallway before I finally came to a door marked with G. Price, who was the Detective who'd occupied Mike Flores' office three Detectives ago. Things like name tags never made much never mind to our local peace keepers. Perhaps because there was so little peace to keep that they had to concentrate not to misplace it.

I knocked and to "Come" went into an office slightly larger than the cleaning closet. It contained a battered metal desk, two fold out chairs facing it. Behind the desk, a stuffed chair, missing its right arm, was full of Mike Flores. Which was hard since Mike Flores was a skinny cuss. He'd tilted the chair back at an angle that I was sure was against specs, but snapped to normal sitting position when I came in and said, "Hey." I didn't know if it was a glad greeting or an oh, you again. Probably between the two.

I shared the coffee and opened the box of jelly doughnuts on the desk. I often did this and dropped by just for a talk when I had the money and nothing was hopping. First, because Mike was one of my oldest friends. And second, because it was good for business. One of the most valuable resources for any PI is a friend – or two – in the police department.

It's not that we solve a ton of murders, or even serious crimes. Well, not at my level it isn't. It's more that, whether you're looking for someone who bailed out on child support, or someone who wrote a bunch of false checks, or even someone who is blackmailing someone's kid, you're likely to find yourself in the unsavory part of town.

Police Detectives have a perfectly sensible belief that if you hang out around the scum of the Earth a lot, there's a good chance you're one of them.

If you don't want to find yourself in a lineup of likely suspects, at least in an Detective's mind, you'll keep friendly relations, and make sure the Detectives know that your business is – most of the time – at the other end of the spectrum from petty thieves, drug dealers and pimps.

The other part of it is that sometimes you do get leads that help you get business. Say they just booked someone for drug dealing. Chances are this person wasn't the cleanest in town and that there are other things that can be traced to him or her, and people who were wronged by them.

If nothing else, if they're of a certain social class, there will be someone looking to divorce them, and perhaps wanting other kinds of evidence to make sure this person doesn't get custody.

So Mike and I were on friendly terms.

Garbled – through chewing a jelly doughnut – platitudes were exchanged, about how great the jelly doughnuts were, and how Jill's coffee was so much better than the stuff in the police station.

"I think they make it with battery acid," Mike said, which wasn't an original observation. Having tasted it, I'm also going to say it probably wasn't wrong, but somehow fell short of the truth. They'd made it with battery acid that had been strained through someone's dirty gym socks.

I empathized, took a swig of my coffee, and after judging enough time and enough friendliness had been expended said, "So, about Schneider."

"Ah. That. It's going to hit the tabloids so hard, Leb. It's not just that it's a murder. Or that it seems to be a ritual murder. It's that it is the weirdest ritual murder I've ever even heard of."

He proceeded to tell me the same stuff Rod had told me. About the drawing on the wall, and the weird misspelled warning, but then he made a face. "The weirdest part?" he said.

"Yeah?"

"There were footprints on the floor." He paused again. "Not human. We haven't had an expert in yet, but one of our guys used to work at the zoo, and he said he could see lion and bear and wolf, but all in one and all … wrong."

"Uh huh," I said. It was probably easy to fake that sort of thing, but what kind of person wore animal-paw shoes to commit a murder?

I mean, sure, I didn't investigate murders. But that was mostly because most murders had nothing whatsoever to investigate. No, really.

Your average, run of the mill murder usually was someone who got mad and shot, stabbed or hit someone else over the head with a blunt object and the most puzzling thing about it all – possibly, in some cases after why – was why the dumb sonofabitch who'd committed it hadn't run, but just sat there – or made a sandwich – until the police that nosy neighbors had called came to arrest him.

I'd brushed around the edges of murder once or twice, when looking for a missing person or a runway. The number of times that had turned into finding a corpse in some field, or worse, blanched bones in someone's car or under some tarps in their yard wasn't more than the number of times I'd actually found the person alive, well, and – usually – stupid, but it was running close to it.

This one though….

Mike had slowed down on his chewing. I didn't disturb him, as he seemed to be deep in thought. He took a swig, and put the coffee cup down on the table. "Wanna see him?" he asked. "The stiff?"

"Sure," I said. "Sure." And finished my jelly doughnut and took a swig of coffee, before putting it down. "I presume there's something you want me to see?"

He nodded, but frowned at the same time. Then stood up, scribbled something on his note pad that I knew, from other occasions, was something like "Morgue. Back soon." And got up.

As normal in our neighborhood – which started German with shades of Scandinavian, changed to Irish, then Italian, and by the time I was born was getting a strong infusion of South American – Mike is an undefinable mix of humanity. His last name is Spanish, his first name is Irish, and judging from his height he had some German in there, even if it was all subsumed in tan skin and black hair so straight it stood up even at two inches of length. But his eyes were green, and his legs way too long. By which I mean I had to run to keep up with him, as we walked through the hallways filled with policemen, secretaries, and other police administration.

If it weren't for the fact that people stopped him with questions about various cases, I'd have got lost, drowned in the sea of humanity, never to be found again.

That's one thing movies and books get wrong about the police. They don't work one case at a time, and a Police Detective doesn't have days to sit around, mooning over some murdered girl or whatever. In a big city like Cleveland, he's usually solving twenty crimes at once, and juggling details in his head, like someone juggling chainsaws. Running chainsaws. Under water.

The other thing books and TV series get wrong is the morgue.

Sure, it has big drawers to store the bodies. The bodies sometimes wear toe tags with a name, or at least the place the body was found and the number of the case it pertains to. Sure, there are stainless steel tables.

But it is neither an hygienically cold place, sterile looking and scientific, nor are the coroner and assistants cold, cerebral people.

The morgue itself doesn't have any décor. It wouldn't unless you wanted the décor to get covered in aerosolized human fat, from the use of rotary cutting implements and other such over many, many years. But the coroner at the Dinkhelsbuhl precinct was a chubby, jovial man.

He didn't wear a white coat. Most coroners don't. They wear scrubs instead, of the sort you see on any nursing assistant, in your local hospital. Those are usually green or blue.

His were black. Because … why not? And in the chest area he had and emblem embroidered with Evil Scientists Union, Local 47 which was probably a made up thing. Probably.

Still, it beat the scrubs his next-in-line assistant wore and which were almost certainly custom made, out of a fabric with big-eyed kittens. Which at the moment were scarier than evil scientists, as far as I was concerned.

They did wear the shower-cap type hair covering, and gloves. And the other assistants looked more normal, though one wore pink scrubs, which in the present circumstances also made me shudder.

The coroner himself, Doctor Diggem – don't blame me, I didn't name him – grinned when he saw Mike. It was a type of grin I'd seen before, though not often. It was the sort of delighted grin a kid would give when he'd just found a particularly interesting type of insect.

Mike didn't actually step back. He just shifted his weight from his front foot to his back one, and his face went to what now? Aloud, in a suspicious voice, like the parent being proffered the self-same interesting insect, he said, "What now, John?"

"Oh, you're going to like this," Doc Diggem said.

"Somehow I doubt it," Mike said.

Doc Diggem nodded to me, then led us to a table in the far corner and pulled the sheet back from Albert Schneider's face. It didn't improve anything. His forehead was indeed carved with a pair of ears, and a smiley face. Which didn't lend any levity to his very pale, waxy-looking skin, or his wide-open, glazed eyes.

Then he pulled the sheet lower, leaving it draped over Albert from the waist down.

Some of it was as I expected, and let me just say that even flabby dead-white skin looked better on the man than pink. But the hole in the middle of his chest didn't.

"Did someone use a rocket launcher on him?" I asked.

Doc Diggem looked serious. "Oh no. His heart and the area around it were... eaten. But then there's this." He made to turn Albert Schneider over, and his assistant with the cat scrubs moved in and helped.

On his back, there were long, parallel marks, like a giant claw – say a lion or bear – had raked his bare back.

I took a deep breath in and held it, and was glad the morgue was so cold. Look, I'm not a sensitive plant. I know that death is rarely pretty, and that anything being investigated as murder was horrible. But something had clawed him, and ... eaten his heart.

"So attack by wild beast?" Mike said. He sounded bored. I suspected the ability to sound bored at the most horrifying developments was something taught in the police academy. "People keep them, you know? Against all rules and laws, people keep lions and bears and tigers and–"

"Oh my," Doctor Diggem said drily. "They sure do. You don't have to tell me that, since most of those who do, or their visitors, end up on my table. But you only wish this were a wild beast attack." He pulled the sheet back the whole way, and on Bertie's butt there were ... human bite marks.

I almost jumped back, in surprise, but I could see the unholy gleam in the doctor's eye, waiting for me to do just that, so of course I wouldn't.

"Schneider was into some kinky stuff?" Mike said, tentatively.

The doctor shook his head. "Probably not," he said. "There are no older marks, which there would be, if he made it a part of his sex life. As far as we can tell these marks were made at or about the time of death. But more importantly–" he paused till Mike prompted him. "Yes?"

"As far as we can tell, the bite marks match the dentition of whoever ate his heart and the area around it."

Now I was going to throw up. I looked at the hole on his chest, which went all the way through. Someone had done that. Someone had ripped human flesh and eaten.... "Did anyone find the parts that were ripped out?" I said.

The doctor looked at me like I was nuts. "No, I said they were eaten," he said.

I moved around to be right under the air conditioning vent, cold air blowing in my face for a while and concentrated on not throwing up.

When I managed to pay attention, Mike was saying, "–don't need all the headlines blaring cannibal murderer."

"Sure," Doctor Diggem said. "But you know it will get out. I have a dozen assistants, and for all I know one of them is married to a journalist. Or has a secret blog. Expect the press to come calling soon."

"Oh, I do," Mike said. "I'll just have to figure out how to tell them as little as possible."

We returned to his office in a subdued mood. He fished in the bag for another jelly doughnut, but I was all right, really. I took a couple of sips of my now cold coffee, and dropped back in the chair.

"You see why I told you it was out of your league?" he asked me.

"Yeah," I said, my voice dry. "Or at least out of my ability to look at and still eat."

He gave me an amused glance.

"I don't suppose it could be gangs?" I said. "I mean, is it possible that this is some kind of tactic to put fear in the heart of snitches, or whatever?"

"If Schneider was involved with gangs, we never heard of it, which would be weird," Mike said. "And besides, I never heard of a raw flesh cannibal cult gang. Some of the Mexican ones do pretty weird things, but not chew all the way through a man's chest and eat it. I don't know if you noticed it, but someone chewed through his ribs. That's like…."

"Steel jaws," I said.

"Something like that. I just keep thinking this embodies biting someone in the ass and eating one's heart out."

"Metaphors?" I said.

He shrugged. "I'm also fairly sure he wasn't killed by a roving gang of English teachers. Probably."

"Mrs. Kaufman was pretty tough," I said, referring to the woman who'd taught us both grammar in high school. "I guess she's been dead for years, though."

It only got him a slight smile, followed by the kind of distant look people get when thinking really hard. "Look, this has bad juju written all over it, Leb. If I were you, I think I'd leave it alone."

I couldn't, of course. The presence of cat ears and what was written on Albert's wall made it solidly part of my case, and I didn't back off from cases, damn it.

"What about whatever's going on with Emma?" I asked.

"Emma?" he said. His face was completely blank. Now, I know that he went to school with Emma, just like I did. So how could he possibly have forgotten her? "Emma Accorso?"

Mike frowned. "From the neighborhood? Sure. I know Emma. What's going on with her?"

At least that was a relief. They've long since stopped having murder divisions in the police – oh, beg your pardon, peace keeper departments. In a sensible move, probably unheard of for any civic institution, they'd made it a "Serious Crimes" department, because sometimes, of course, kidnapping or blackmailing or something turned into murder, and it was good to have some continuity of investigation.

So one of the many cases Mike was dealing with might have been the kidnapping of Lilly Michal Jones.

I just didn't want to think Mike – who was pretty solid as a Police Detective – was considering Emma as a real suspect. Because if he were, then there might be something behind the suspicion. And I didn't want to consider it. I'd just recovered Emma from possible marriage to a dentist, and wasn't ready to lose her to she was a murderer after all. I mean, I'd probably never date her – I'd have to find the courage to ask her out first – and the way things were, our acquaintance would probably never even be real friendship. But at least for a while, I'd be able to have my image of her restored and the hope that I'd somehow find the courage to ask her out. Because miracles can happen, right?

I realized I could stomach a doughnut again, and grabbed one, so I had something to do, when I said "Lilly Michal Jones' disappearance."

"What? What does Emma have to do with that?"

I told him about my morning phone call. Mike looked stunned for a moment, then snarled, "That asshole."

"Emma?" I said.

"No, not Emma. Joe Scarlati. I didn't even realize he was doing that. That's insane!"

I conjured up an image from high school. He'd been class president, captain of the football team, and all around golden boy. About a foot taller than my 5'7",", dark blond, blue eyed, and definitely someone who was made in a factory. A factory that made very tall men. "I thought he was in computers?"

"Sure. He was. But his company crashed and he decided he wanted to do something for the community. At last that's what he says. He became a Detective, and is bucking hard for promotion. He's investigating the Jones case, and man … he's practically kissing the parents' feet."

"Huh?"

"The kid's parents. Harrington-Jones. They're pieces of work. And in my opinion they should be prime suspects. But apparently they go to the same parties as Scarlati. Or something. So be refuses to even consider them, even though the house was a mess of contaminated evidence and we're ninety percent sure the mother got rid of the kid's clothes and stuffed animals to make it look like she'd come back for them."

To my blank look, he said, "Two days after she disappeared, most of her clothes disappeared from her closet, and also three stuffed kittens and two teddy bears."

I blinked. "She could be a runway, you know?" the idea terrified me. A little innocent kid out there on the streets of Cleveland would neither stay innocent nor probably alive for very long.

"Yeah, we know, and we're making all the enquiries, but this is just weird. Emma often took the kid after school, and until the parents got home. As far as I could tell, she never got paid, either, and the parents didn't care, except for being glad the kid went there. Saved them paying someone to watch her. But now they keep saying she's a dangerous spinster, jealous of their lives and their having a family. At first they said she must have helped Lilly run away, then they said she must have kidnapped Lilly. Emma let us look all over her house. Well, not me, but you know, the department. And then the parents said that she must have killed the kid." He sounded disgusted.

"Yeah," I said, "and buried her in the backyard."

"Which is nonsense. It's a tiny backyard, overlooked by three neighbors. You know, her mom's house. She would never be so crazy as to think she could get away with burying a kid there." He rubbed his forehead, as if he had a headache come on. "The worst part of it? Emma is in a pretty bad place, you know, looking after her mom. She doesn't need this. She's looked after her mom for ten years, and all of us on the block keep an eye on them, in case something goes wrong."

"You live on the same block?"

He nodded. "Three doors down." He looked sheepish. "Okay, so she takes little Mike and Joana after school too, and yeah, she won't let us pay her, so we do things for her, like mow the lawn, and look after her mom when Emma has to go to the doctor, and stuff. Look, Emma is good people." He took an almost ferocious bite of a new jelly doughnut. "Yeah, sure, we know she takes those kids in after school as a form of amusement for herself, maybe compensation for the kids she never got to have, the life she never got to live, but she's still good people, and she helps the kids with homework and all. It's a good thing she's doing. Then Lilly disappeared, the parents started raising a stink, and all of a sudden people are afraid to let the kids go there, and she's down from 8 to our two. And she's heart broken."

I finished my coffee. "I'm going to go there," I said, announcing it like it was some great act of courage. "To stay with her while her backyard is dug up."

I don't know what I expected: resistance or a pat on the back.

Instead, I got approval. "Good, someone should." He paused. "I always thought you two would end up together. I guess it didn't work out. But I'm glad she can still count on you."

He got up to shake my hand, though we normally didn't do that. And I was rewarded for my trouble as I got nearer to shake his hand. You see, Albert Schneider's file was still on the desk, open, face up. And there were a bunch of notes on the corner, including "Pupper Cuddles" and a name: Brian Lee Gnad.

Well, then. Mike would never tell me those names, since he thought I was way out of my league – and thinking of how Albert had died, he might very well be right – but maybe he wanted me to see those.

Driving over to Emma's, I thought that I could get the band's details from Rando.

Emma lived deep in the old neighborhood. I lived in the next neighborhood over, because I could never afford the place I'd grown up in. My foster parents had sold their house when they went into a nursing home, and even though it was then well over 100 years old and had fifty years of delayed maintenance, the price had been more than I'd make in 20 years.

Dinkhelsbuhl had been founded at the turn of the 19th century by dour, hardworking German immigrants. Their influence remained behind in the houses that lined the central streets: squarish looking Victorians, with very little ornamentation and steep roofs, giving the impression they'd been transported wholesale from some Alpine village. It was impossible to drive through Dinkhelsbuhl and not think at any moment the burgmeister would emerge from his door to investigate the case of the pied piper.

It had stayed German and Scandinavian for about thirty years, after which Irish and Italian immigrant families had moved in. You could see traces of them in the Catholic church up the street, its interior all Carrera marble, imported from the old country, its architecture flamboyant-Mediterranean, all spires and towers in small scale, making it look like a shrunk-down Cathedral. There were also a couple of Italian restaurants that went back almost 100 years, run by the same families: Bazolli's family restaurant, and Gino's Trattoria.

The area had started to go downhill – like many urban areas – somewhere around the sixties, but it had been on the upswing since the nineties, heralded by a few brave people moving in and painting and fixing the houses, followed by edgy art galleries and restaurants, still around, followed up by more people who wanted to live somewhere exciting – but not too exciting – until now the old fashioned bones of the place were overlaid by cutting-edge artsy murals painted on the sides of the old gas stations, now restaurants, and the old dry cleaners, now coffee shops.

Emma's block remained mostly residential, with the homes painted in every color of the rainbow, and women in carefully tailored jeans creating miniature perfection in their handkerchief-sized front yards. The only exception was at the corner where there used to be a small grocery store: Benini's. It had been torn down some time ago, and in its place rose a ten story glass-and-steel condo building, which housed people like Harrington-Jones, who wanted to live urban and "happening" but not to grovel in the mud with the rest of humanity, or be so close they could see people on the street, and watch the old residents greet each other.

Emma's place fit in with the others, which must mean she'd devoted her time to the front yard. In place of the sloping lawn with a couple of overgrown hydrangea bushes I remembered from childhood, where were now steps, and mini-terraces, creating flower beds. I didn't know the name for any of the flowers, but most of them were blooming, causing a cacophony of contrasting color and form.

I started up the stone steps, and stopped, because there was a white haired woman, sitting on the porch swing. "Mrs. Accorso," I said, recognizing Emma's mom, even if she was fifteen years older, and had a strangely vacant look in her eyes.

The vacant eyes slowly turned towards me, and even while looking at me straight on seemed to be coming from a long way away. Finally, she said, and it was a question. "Magis?"

I blinked. "Yes," I said, shocked she remembered me, but she undid it in the next sentence, "How is Leb doing? He hasn't come over in a long time. We miss him."

I realized, as though she'd said it, that she thought she was talking to my father. She was seeing me, but in her mental map, I was Dad coming by to … who knew? I knew from old pictures I looked like Dad. But that was my bio dad. Not my foster dad. And I only knew it from pictures, because I didn't actually remember my real dad. I'd been too young when he died. I knew we'd lived in the neighborhood, because my foster family had told me so.

Now I realized that Emma's mom must have known my parents, known Dad, though she'd never talked about it to me, or at least not that I remembered.

Had Dad dropped by? Dropping in on the neighbors, to borrow the lawnmower or something like that, was pretty normal when I was growing up.

"I suppose you want to talk to Joe," Mrs. Accorso said. "He should be in the back, in the workshop."

Mr. Accorso had been dead by the time Emma and I were in high school. I remembered the funeral. "Bring Lebby to play, sometime."

I cleared my throat, staying rooted on the steps, not knowing how to respond. How do you talk to someone who is in a completely different place and time? How do you reach them? What do you say?

"Well, yes. He … he's busy," I managed.

And that's when Emma opened the screen door, and saw me. "Leb!" she said. She gave something like a squeak, and then she was hugging me. Which made me even more confused than her mom's thinking I was my dad. "Leb, I'm so glad you've come!"

She seemed to realize that she was hugging me, and stepped back, still smiling, and now blushing.

At thirty five, Emma looked pretty much like she had at eighteen. Her red hair was tied back, her green eyes sparkled, and she had a quirky smile, and a splash of freckles across her nose. She hadn't gained weight, quite the contrary. And if there were marks of strain and fine wrinkles on her features, which of us had escaped youth unchanged?

"You look the same," she said, and I repressed a desire to reach up and cover my receding hairline.

"Yeah, well," I said, and looked sideways towards Mrs. Accorso, who had gone back to staring blankly ahead.

"She's okay," Emma said. "Really. Come inside. We'll be just in the front hall. There's someone coming to help. Mrs. Flores from down the block, you know?"

"I know. I talked to her husband, Mike, earlier."

"They're very nice," she said. "I keep the kids when she needs to shop and stuff, and she keeps an eye on Mom when I have to do something. She said she'd come by and stay while the police are here, but I'm so glad you've come."

The next five minutes, standing in her cool front hall, still sparsely furnished, with just the same bench and hat rack her mom had had there when we were kids, we caught each other up. Her story was what I'd heard before, except for her saying that the first five years she'd lived with her mom, she'd been able to have part time jobs, just to get out of the house. Her mom had been having memory issues, and losing things, but it had not become serious "till she started giving the houseplant milk, and watering the cat. Not to mention the time she gave the UPS delivery man a thousand dollars for a tip. Then I couldn't afford to work outside the house, you know?"

Mine? Well, how do you tell the story of giving up? I'd finished high school and taken an Associates in Business and, after not finding any work – it had been a bad time for work around here – had taken training as a PI and started doing the sort of thing I did now. "Sometimes it's feast," I said. "But it's mostly famine. And mostly when I'm doing well, I save for when business is slow."

She nodded and smiled, her eyes sparkling, "But it must be interesting, sometimes?"

I shrugged. "Sometimes," I said. And sometimes the most interesting part of the month was figuring out how to pay my rent. But I never got to expound on it, as Mrs. Flores showed up, with her youngest daughter on her hip, and said she'd watch Mrs. Accorso.

This was just before Dinkhelsbuhl's finest showed up. They were headed by Joe Scarlatti, who showed the search warrant to Emma, who went pale and tight lipped. And then we followed the police to the backyard.

Joe Scarlatti really looked like he thought of himself as Dinkhelsbuhl's finest. He must have spent his morning in front of the mirror, getting his hair to curve up just so. And he wore a suit that was much more expensive than what most policemen could afford. Let's assume he'd got it in his days of making a lot more than policemen made.

As for the broomstick that seemed to have got up his bum, it might have been a congenital thing. I had a vague memory of his father looking like that when he picked us up from school: nose in the air and shoulders very square, as though he were doing us a favor by coming near us.

I expected him to look at Emma with suspicion, but he didn't even do that, just as if she were beneath his notice. And his lip actually curled slightly in disgust when he noticed me, as though I had some kind of deodorant failure, which I damn well hadn't.

The backyard brought back my nostalgia. It was exactly as it had been when we were kids, maybe all of fifty feet wide, but two hundred feet deep. Surrounded by a brick wall that divided it from the other gardens around here, the walls were as I'd always known them, covered in ivy. The center was thick lawn, but around the edges there were flower beds, and some of them were obviously newly planted with rose bushes. The police concentrated on these.

"I'm not going to have the money to replace them," Emma said, absently, while they dug into the flowerbeds. "I planted them because Mom had roses around her childhood garden and kept asking me why they didn't grow."

For a long time it went on, with the police digging and Joe Scarlatti standing in the middle supervising. He wore a good quality suit, and looked as if he thought he owned the place. He was the sort of guy you hated on sight.

The other Detectives, to give them credit, looked embarrassed and acted with all possible politeness. Also, they were pretty careful with Emma's roses. They picked them up and laid them carefully on the lawn. I wondered if that was Mike's influence.

No kid came to light, needless to say. But when they left there was no apology. Joe Scarlatti, instead, stood there and lectured Emma on how she'd encouraged Lilly to disobey her parents, and how if Emma hear from Lilly she should tell the police immediately.

I wanted to punch him, but I knew the kind of trouble you could get into for punching an Detective. Also, I would need a step stool.

Instead, I waited till they were gone, and Emma was crying quietly. I went through the house, and asked Mrs. Flores, "I don't suppose you could stay till the evening?"

She looked surprised, but mumbled something about calling Mike. She pulled out her cellphone and walked into the next room, then came back, all smiles. "He says it's fine."

After a while, Mike drove up, and took their kid, and Mrs. Flores said she'd stay.

By then, Emma had come onto the front porch and said, "Why? I can look after Mom now."

"Nope," I told her. "Let's replant those rose bushes. Maybe they'll survive."

She looked like she was going to cry again, but went back with me, and unlocked the under-the-back-porch space to take out the shovels.

While we worked, she talked to me about Lilly, "She's so bright, you know, but she never really had any education worth the name. No, I don't mean learning things. She learned things. I said she's very bright. But her parents never taught her anything, or even told her it's wrong to do some things.

"When she first started coming here, she used to just take stuff from the other kids when she wanted it. It took learning to like me, to know she was doing something wrong, you know? She thought that there was no wrong or right. No, I misspeak, she felt there was no wrong or right, because no one had ever told her anything she did was wrong or right.

"It makes me so mad. Her parents treat her exactly as if she were an expensive kind of toy poodle or something. I wish they had got those instead. Poodles rarely grow up to be mass murderers."

"Ah. That's because you never met Fluffy, my great aunt's poodle," I'd answered while we patted the dirt around the last rose bush.

We watered all of them, and then at my insistence we went out to Gino's Trattoria, for one of their large sausage and pepperoni pies. And it was sitting across from each other, at the tiniest of tables, the dim light augmented by a candle on a wine bottle between us, that I said, "What you said about Lilly earlier: I don't even know how to ask this, considering she's only six, but I've heard of things kids do … you don't think she's doing something awful?"

Emma's green eyes were serious in the candle light. "I don't know," she said. "I don't even know she would know what wrong was. I think, honestly, as quickly as she became fond of me, just because I showed her some attention, she could be led to do just about anything from stealing to drug running by someone who paid her a little attention. And I don't know what was going on in the days before she disappeared, but she was talking about having a secret, and about this funny guy she met. Now she was a very imaginative child, and since she told me had a face like a dolphin's and ears like a cabbage, I thought it was just some imaginary thing she was talking about. I never thought to worry until she disappeared. And, oh, Leb, I think part of the reason her parents think I had something to do with this is that I didn't ask her more questions, or figure out what she was up to, so I feel guilty and they pick up on that."

"I think the reason her parents think you had something to do with this is because they're assholes," I said, and it was my deep, well-reasoned conclusion.

I walked her back from the Trattoria, under the maple trees that lined each side of the street. We didn't kiss at the door. We'd never kissed at the door. At best we'd been friends. And now, after all these years, we were mere acquaintances, even if she'd hugged me when she'd first seen me.

I wanted to kiss her at the door, but instead, I'd said good night, and she'd said, "Wait, Leb. Thank you so much for being here for me."

"Anytime," I said, tipping an imaginary hat at her. And then I'd waited till she was in the house, and I'd heard her talk to Mrs. Flores, before I headed to my car.

This is all I could hope for just now. And just for now, it was good. At least I'd got to see her. And there was no dentist. Or any other husband, standing between us. It's not like I had something in particular against dentists, but I was glad she wasn't married. Even if in the end it didn't do me any good. I could dream. Sometimes, dreams are all you need. Or at least they're better than nothing.

4 PUPPER CUDDLES AND PRIEST LARVAE

MY LITTLE RATTY APARTMENT SEEMED EXTRA RATTY AS I CAME IN. How come I'd never noticed the sofa sagged, and the carpet was in dire need of cleaning? Most of all, it looked lonely. Very very lonely. I was grateful that I was going on to 48 hours without sleep, because I just fell into bed and slept, the sleep of the entirely exhausted.

But not without dreams. In my dreams I was running from a guy wearing a suit, like Joe Scarlatti's. Except the guy's face was like a shark's, and he had ears like a cabbage cut in half.

I woke up with my phone buzzing in my pocket. And realized I'd forgotten to undress, or even remove the keys and phone from pockets.

In my still-mostly-asleep state, I got on the phone, and said, "Is that a buzz in my pocket, or are you just happy to see me?"

"What?" Rod Rando's voice said. "What the hell are you talking about, Leb? Have you looked into Albert Schneider's death at all?"

Look, if I'd been fully awake, I'd never have told him, but I wasn't fully awake. A look at the phone told me it was 8 am, which meant I'd slept ten hours, but I still felt as though the confusion of my dream had followed me. I said, "Yeah. I saw his corpse. Someone – human, or at least with human teeth – chewed through the center of his chest, ribs, heart and all. And ate it. They didn't find any pieces. And he wasn't covered in glitter, so likely it wasn't a six year old girl. But there were claw marks, so a lolcat might have been at the scene."

"What?"

And that's when I realized I'd been still half asleep. I woke myself up forcefully, and told Rando about my efforts on his case, as I was making coffee. I didn't even get an attaboy when I told him about the names I'd read on the file. Instead, he growled at Pupper Cuddles. Growled loud enough I wasn't sure he wouldn't have chewed through my ribs and heart if I'd been right there. "Their band name," he said, in a voice that sounded like he'd like to do just that, "is Brütal Wülfsex, damn it. I thought they were too smart to go to the pink."

"Uh huh," I said and didn't even chuckle. Okay, I had to drink a big gulp of coffee to avoid chuckling. But I try not to kick music agents when they're down. Or even when they're up. He did give me the name of the club at which the newly pink Pupper Cuddles played, and the address of two of the band members. Then I asked, "What about this Gnad character?"

"Oh, hell. Brian Lee Gnad was, thank God, never my headache, but I've heard. I mean, hell, everyone has. He and his buddies started this band. It wasn't very good. I mean their greatest hit was Initiate Peach, and that went big only because no one could understand what the hell the lyrics were about. And by greatest hit, I mean they got played a couple of times, by a local radio station. AM. Part of it you know, they called themselves Punk Sausage. I mean, it's not like you're going to get anywhere with that kind of silliness. And then something spooked them. I mean, the band."

"And they called themselves Pink Wiener?"

"No. Nothing like that. At least that would be … well, like the rest of these people. Instead, they split up, and Brian Lee Gnad went back to the seminary."

I swallowed coffee, fast, and coughed as it went the wrong way. As soon as I recovered, I said, "He went back where?"

"The seminary. He was in seminary, you know, to become a Catholic priest, and then became the vocalist for Punk Sausage. Then something scared him so much, he went back. Wait, I remember the name of the seminary, Mary of the Pines. You know, over across from…."

I'd jotted down the address, wondering what kind of person goes from wanting to be a priest to singing in a band and back again. I guess I would find out. That's the thing about the PI business. You find out lots of things. Mostly things you never wanted to know.

This time I managed to shower faster, and I put on my normal jeans, but a newish T-shirt. I mean, I might still somehow run into Emma.

Okay, fine, I'll admit it, I was hoping to see her, even if I had to go and knock at her door again. In fact, I didn't think I could stop myself from doing it. Because I was a sad case, and it was useless to deny that I loved her as much as ever.

But first I had to deal with Pupper Cuddles and this Brian Gnad character.

Rando had said he was fairly sure Pupper Cuddles would be rehearsing at their normal club, the Iron Rose on Pythagoras Road. So I headed there. I'd looked them up and they were okay. Had a couple of albums for sale. Their metal stuff, of course. "They were this close to a major deal," Rando had said. "And then this stuff…."

Approaching the club's side door, I could tell that they were a cut above.

Look, seriously, if you're going to go to the pink, you should at least sound like one of the better K-pop bands. And they did. They were singing about "playing fetch with my puppy" or at least that was the chorus.

I flashed my pass to the door guard, who nodded, "Rando called," he said, in a whisper. His eyes turned back, with something between horror and fascination, to the stage. On the stage—

No matter how many metal bands I saw who had gone to the pink, or even the deepest pink, I could never get used to it.

I'd guess these guys had changed over recently, because they still had shaved heads and walrus moustaches that would do entire tribes of walruses proud.

There were three of them. Drummer-and-vocalist – and who thought that was a good arrangement? – wore a pink T-shirt with a cartoon puppy on it. A cartoon girl puppy. You could tell by the bow and the eyelashes. It was obviously too small to fit him, and stretched in all directions.

The guy on the guitar had a pink T-shirt, but had gone the extra step of having pink butterfly hairclips on either side of his moustache.

The third guy, fooling around with something at that back, was dressed all in pink. Let me just say that no one – no one – should wear pink jeans, if they're male and over the age of six.

Just as they stopped singing about playing fetch and slobbery puppy kisses, I got up to the drummer, flashed the pass and said, "Butcher?"

He had reached for a towel from near the drums, and wiped at his forehead while he blinked at me, in confusion. "Huh? Oh. We ... I call myself Puppy Treats now."

"Uh huh. Puppy Treats." I cleared my throat, because I had the impression they would have no sense of humor whatsoever about this, and my laughing would be taken very badly indeed. "I see. Well ... I understand you knew ... er... Albert Schneider. I mean Sparkle Love Fun."

"Bertie?" the other guy asked. He came closer, and leaned over to shake my hand. "Hi, I'm Wagging Tail. Used to be Slutcrusher. What has Bertie done now?"

"Died," I said. "Or rather was killed. I'm trying to figure out who did it."

Wagging Tail straightened too fast, and looked at me. "He was killed? By whom?"

"As I said, I'm trying to figure that out."

"Oh. But he was all right two days ago. I talked to him. He was trying to buy candles for ... for his appeasement."

I thought of the altar with Hello Kitty. As much as it would please me to make her the murderer—

"And you don't know anyone who'd want to kill him?"

"Maybe his band members," Puppy Treats said. "I mean, Bertie was ... flexible over showing up for engagements. Drove them nuts. Cost them a bunch of money. Every time they were starting to gain some momentum, he'd let them down again. I think it was his taking the whole Satanism thing seriously."

"You mean you don't?" I said.

"Oh, hell no," Puppy Treats said. "It's all a front, you know. The fans love it."

The third guy had come near. I ran my gaze over the expanse of pink jeans, then back at the other two. "So, do they love the pink?"

Wagging Tail sat down, heavy, on the side of the stage. "You have to understand, we're artists. Not everything is commercial. Sometimes you just feel it in your heart that you have to change; that you have to start producing something different. Otherwise you stagnate, man. I mean, you change because you have to, even if it costs you money."

"Like Van Gogh," Puppy Treats said. "I mean, he made stuff no one wanted to buy ... then, but now he's like all famous and stuff."

"I ain't cutting my ear off," the third guy said.

"No one asked you to!" Wagging Tail said, impatiently.

"No one is cutting anyone's ear," Puppy Treats said. He looked back at me. "We don't take it that seriously. We just felt we had to change our look. For ... for our art."

"It's the dreams, man," Puppy Treats looked abashed.

"Dreams?"

"We all started having these horrible dreams. It was like teddy bear picnic in Hell, with all these weird demons, and threats and stuff. When we went to the pink, it stopped. It just stopped and we could actually sleep. You don't know what a difference that makes."

"Of course I do," I said. "I'm a PI."

They didn't ask me what that had to do with anything, which tells you how shell shocked they were, right there.

I couldn't get anything else out of them. They weren't as deeply into that Satanist stuff as Albert Schneider. In fact, they said they weren't into it at all. It was all an artistic decision, and now they'd made another decision. And that was about it.

Feeling slightly disappointed – but what had I expected them to tell me, really? Particularly after Albert Schneider's end, and I'd bet they knew about it, because the community had telepathic-speed communications – I drove towards Mary of the Pines Seminary, on the edge of town.

First, I was surprised at the place, both location and appearance. Edge of town means it was located just off a massively industrial neighborhood, with abandoned warehouses that had once served the needs of tire factories, and some remaining factories that I couldn't tell if they were active or not. I suppose given an influx of population, and better economics, it would become a trendy neighborhood, with restaurants in every warehouse, and bars in every factory. But that's not the way it looked now. It looked like a blighted landscape, and almost deserted, except for fleeting shadows disappearing into alleyways. It was the sort of place where I'd hate for my car to break down.

And then I took one of those alleys, to the left, and suddenly the warehouses stopped. There was a bridge, and a place that looked like a toxic dump of industrial machinery, and then suddenly straggly trees, and then just as suddenly a manicured lawn, and a white building, next to a church.

The change was so sudden I looked behind me, to make sure I hadn't dreamed the blighted area and wasn't dreaming this.

There was one path leading to the church, and then a sign pointing to the right saying "Mary of the Pines Seminary." And another path that followed around the white building. I walked the path. It went through a manicured vegetable garden with a sign saying "Community garden" and something about 100% of the produce being donated to the soup kitchen, and then around again, to another building behind that one.

This one was probably older. It was brick, two stories, and built in that square-with-a-hole-in-the-middle plan that most high schools in the seventies were.

But when I knocked at the door, and it opened, I wasn't in a high school atrium, but in a small, clean front hall, that smelled of floor wax, and had two benches, one on each side. It looked more like Emma's entrance hall than like an institutional anything.

The lady who'd opened the door to me, and who wore a grey dress, smiled at me, "How may we help you?" she asked. I got a strong suspicion she was a nun. How are you supposed to tell them these days when most of them don't even wear headdresses?

"I would like to see Brian Lee Gnad. It's important." I felt suddenly embarrassed. Did you call Seminarians Father or Brother or something? I had no idea. My parents had been Catholic, and I'd been baptized, but they'd died when I was six. I remembered, of what they'd taught me, only two prayers, both of them suitable for really small kids. I hadn't prayed in much too long. My foster parents, who'd actually brought me up, hadn't been religious. And while I don't think they'd have objected to my continuing Catholic education, I was too young to ask for it, and not one else had. So I'd never learned more about religion than I'd known at six. Certainly no one had told me what one should call priests in training. Priestlings? Larval priests? Almost certainly not the latter. Probably not the former, either.

The lady in the gray dress was looking at me, speculatively, like she was trying to figure out something, "How important? And what does it pertain to?"

"It's ... it's ...." I considered wildly telling her it was a family secret, or that I was looking for the key to stop the nuke exploding, or something, but there were probably extra rules about lying to a nun. I'm on a mission from God, would also be a lie. Probably. And I was already in enough trouble. One thing was to be afraid of being damned for eternity, since no human being can quite picture eternity. But these days, the evil side of things seemed to be going for using deep pink, and/or chewing people's chests out as a punishment. I thought of poor Bertie Schneider, and shook my head. I certainly didn't want to end up like that. "I'm here at the behest of a man named Rod Rando, whom he knows. I'm helping investigate someone's murder."

Her eyebrows went up, while I tried to think whether saying I was investigating the murder counted as a lie. I mean, it wasn't precisely what I was investigating, right? I was trying to figure out why Rod Rando's clients were sounding like little Korean girls and singing about puppy cuddles and kitten kisses.

But Rando was freaked out about Schneider's murder, too. And besides, it was probable that whoever had killed Rando also knew about the pink stuff.

The woman nodded. Perhaps she had come to the conclusion that I was truthful. Because who'd make up something that weird? Or perhaps the freaked out truth-rays of my absolute scare at this stuff had communicated itself to her. She said, "Come with me."

I went with her, along a long corridor, and into a small room, that looked exactly like a living room, only not my living room, because the sofa and chair, and coffee table in it were all new and clean, and rested on a burgundy rug that looked like one of those "hemmed pieces of carpet" that carpet mills sell, but which was also clean.

Behind the sofa was a painting of an angel walking behind a boy and a girl who are about to walk off a precipice. I sat in the chair and glared at it. If angels didn't sneak up on the kids, the kids would probably look where they were walking. The whole thing looked like a prank, with the angel going "Ha ha, look what I made you do," except that the angel looked all serious and sad. A plaque underneath it said St. Raphael. Probably the angel, not the artist. Or at least, I'd never yet learned of a painter being a saint. And I figured I would have on novelty alone.

Someone cleared his throat and I got up, reflexively.

Brian Lee Gnad was a round faced young man, maybe 30, with light brown hair and beard, and sparkling eyes, that looked amused, as though I'd done something very funny. He spoke in a well-modulated voice, "I am sorry for interrupting your contemplation," he said.

"I wasn't contemplating," I said, and my voice sounded unexpectedly surly.

He smiled and glanced over his shoulder at the picture, but didn't say anything. Instead, he gestured for me to sit down, and sat down on the sofa, close to the chair. He wore dark pants and a white shirt, which might very well be normal, except I'd been expecting white robes or something. "Sister Mary said you were here about a murder?" He was frowning slightly.

I didn't say, Ah, I knew she was a nun, but I felt every bit as victorious as if I had. On the heels of that, I felt a little surprised that he also hadn't been seen by the police, and wondered in what context and why they'd put those names on the file. Was Mike sending me on a fool's errand, to keep me away from the real murder investigation? I wouldn't put it past him. If nothing else because as long as I stayed alive, there was a chance I'd bring him more jelly doughnuts.

"It's about a man named Albert Schneider," I said.

"Bertie Schneider?" He seemed genuinely surprised. I guessed at this point he wouldn't be part of the community. He opened his mouth, and looked like he was about to say something. Then closed it. "He died? Really?"

I nodded, "He was murdered."

Brian sat down. "Poor soul." And, at my look, he added, "He wasn't a bad man, you know? Despite all the silly affectations and Satanism stuff." A pause. "Or maybe I'm wrong. Recently I–" He shrugged. "Look, I barely knew him. I don't know what I can tell you about him, or whoever killed him. I mean, I'm not exactly one of his bosom buddies. My friends and I, well, we were mostly playing at it, and when push came to shove, we just gave it up and went back to … to our normal callings, before we started playing at being a band."

I organized my thoughts. I can, too. Though you might suspect that my mental cubbyholes are very strangely arranged, and you won't be too far wrong. "It's about the pink," I said. And I started telling him everything. I expected him to interrupt me, and tell me I was out of my mind, but he didn't. He listened gravely, frowning a little.

Once or twice, I thought he was going to say something, but he didn't. Instead, he continued frowning while I told him everything, including the horrible way Bertie Schneider had died and the lolcat message scribbled in his own blood on the wall.

He looked grave and sat in silence a while after I was done talking, then said, "Wait a moment."

I waited while he got up and left the room. I heard his steps sounding down the hallway, in the other direction from which I'd come. A while after, I heard him approach again.

He sat down on the sofa, and put a laptop on the coffee table, then sat down and fooled with it for a while. Then he looked up, and all amusement was gone from his face. "You remember what you said about dreams? Well, Punk Sausage was a very minor band, on the fringes of the entire scene. We used to joke we had like five fans, and they showed up every night at the bar, and if they all could get plus ones, we could double our fandom. We might or might not have joked about getting them all to marry and have kids, so we could quadruple our fandom." He smiled, but it didn't last. "But then, suddenly, we also started having bad dreams. Nightmares, just like, you know, Brütal Wülfsex. I ... perhaps because of my education, I saw it like being lost in a Hieronimus Bosch painting. I thought we were being pursued by demons in our dreams, and told at the same time that we were supposed to wear pink clothes and play things about puppies and kittens." He paused. "I thought we were going nuts."

"And?" I said, thinking of the shark-headed thing in my dreams.

"And in the middle of it all, the weird thing is that there was this little redheaded girl, and she insisted on holding teas, with all these demons and damned souls. You know, the cutest little girl you've ever seen, with red pigtails, and a splash of freckles, and jeans and a T-shirt with a kitten."

My mind flashed onto an image of Lilly. But she'd only been missing for two weeks. It couldn't possibly be her. This had been going on for two years. It couldn't be Lilly. Right?

Gnad shook his head. "Anyway, it was all pretty scary, even with the little girl. Perhaps more so because of the little girl. You know?"

I didn't, but I nodded as if I did. "So, in the middle of all this, while some of the guys are saying that maybe we should play some music about pink or kittens or puppies or teddy bears or something, just to make it all go away, we were sitting around late one evening, and we might have had more than a couple of beers each, and I told them I didn't want to do it, because the whole thing felt unclean to me. I'm not sure I can explain."

"I'd appreciate it if you'd try," I said.

"Well, it felt ... wrong." He squirmed. "I probably could explain it to you under the same principles that the Catholic Church uses to invalidate "false visions." Do you understand those? Are ... are you Catholic?"

I shook my head. "I think I was baptized," I said, "But my parents died when I was six. Car accident. All I have left of Mom that relates to religion is this little medal from Fatima that says In Fatima I prayed for you, so I assume either she or her parents went there. And after that I had a foster family. They were okay, but I don't think they were particularly religious so I was never educated in any of this stuff."

He opened his mouth, closed it, then nodded. "Okay. Well, then you don't know, but you've heard of apparitions of the Virgin Mary?"

I dug into my pocket. Look, it was the only thing I had from Mom. I always carried it. It was a little silver, oval medal, with an image of the virgin appearing to the shepherds and inscribed on the back. I showed it to him on my palm and said, "I read up on it. My mom always wore this. I remember it. So when I was old enough to read it, I read up on it."

He nodded. "So, if you read up on it, you probably heard of other apparitions of the Virgin."

"Like Lourdes. Sure. I once dated a girl named Mary Lourdes."

"Right. But what you probably don't know is that for every real apparition there are several fake ones."

"Fake?" I said. "You mean, people lying about having seen Mary?"

He shook his head. "Not … quite. Oh, sure there are plenty of those, and sometimes they get going for a while, but those are more a … a supermarket tabloid type of thing. Mary sends a woman letters or perhaps emails type of thing. The Church never gets involved.

"No, the difficult ones are where there is something not quite natural going on. People weigh a ton one minute, don't weigh anything the next, or perhaps they fall into deep trances and prophesy."

"Wouldn't those all be real?"

He looked thoughtful. "No. They are real in the sense that the people experiencing them aren't actually lying, and believe they have seen the Virgin, or angels or the saints. But they are not real in the sense that they're supernatural, i.e. belonging to a realm above humans and working through the action of God or his elect. I mean to the extent that everything that exists does so by God's will, it–" He took a deep breath. "Okay, let me try not to get myself tangled up in definitions and you along with me. Let's posit that the realms we can see, hear or understand the action of are the natural, i.e. they're subjected to the laws of physics. Things can be scientifically explained, even if we don't always know the explanation."

"Okay," I said. "But–"

He held up a hand. "No, listen. I know it gets all tangled up between can be explained and we can explain them right now, or … all that stuff. To a savage, the operation of a radio, say, or a cell phone is not natural, and even the rest of us know only that they're natural by fiat. Most of us could no more explain in detail how they work than we could fly unassisted. It was this type of thing that drove me from … from my training, and from belief, even, for a while." He shook his head. "Until I experienced something that couldn't be natural. You know the difference, trust me on this, when you actually experience it.

"Anyway, so here's where we are. The natural world is what most of us think of as the world, in its totality. Then there is the preternatural world. Ghosts. Fairies, dragons. All the refugees of urban fantasy. I don't know if you believe in them. In the long run it doesn't matter if you believe in them, just as it doesn't matter if you believe in the supernatural. Reality is that which continues to exist even if you don't believe in it.

"And yeah, I know most people who believe in that call it supernatural, but it's not really. In a way it is 'natural' in the sense that it was created by God, for purposes not in our ken. I suppose if we studied it … well, eventually we'd figure out how it works and why, and might even learn to control it. Sure we've failed so far, but so did we fail at understanding electricity for so long that we worshipped gods of the thunderbolt."

I was lagging about a million miles behind, my mind snagged on one point, "Wait, are you saying you believe in ghosts, dragons, fairies and … and all that rot?" I know I said earlier I don't really believe in God. Not the way other people do. But even He was easier to believe in – even if not understandable – than the idea that Tolkien was right all along.

He smiled. "Well, I haven't made a study of it, but after experiencing some things.... Look, the Church tends to assume that everyone who is not explicitly on the side of good, angels and emissaries of God, are evil, or in league with the other side.

"I'm not sure it's that simple. There seem to be other things going on, along with the natural world, other parts of created reality that are … well, not even concerned with us. They exist in their way for purposes of their own, like the dinosaurs before humans."

"I though religious people didn't believe–"

"No. Catholics believe in evolution. We just believe God directed it. Probably behind the scenes and with the occasional thumb on the scales. Seems to be His style. Anyway, all that stuff we don't understand would be capable of some preternatural effects. Effects that we don't understand yet, and that affect our world in a way beyond the reality we understand. And by we, I mean even scientists. Did you know for instance that people all have something like eye infections both after encounters with fairies and encounters with UFOs? Or that there are resemblances between the two experiences?"

I almost said Oh, Jesus because the last thing I was worried about was UFOs or fairies. If those existed in any sense, super or peter or Bob or Joe or whatever. But I assumed quasi-religious exclamations would be taken the wrong way, so I just said, "Huh."

"Right, right," he said, and I had a feeling he had been rebuked for over-explaining or getting lost in the weeds before. "Never mind that. The point is that there are apparitions where something weird is going on but that the Church decides aren't really supernatural, meaning from heaven, that is, above nature, because of various reasons. Some of those reasons are frivolity, for instance. God, his mother or his angels wouldn't come interact with humans just to say oh, hai hooman."

"Please," I said. "lolcats are not funny right now."

"Okay," he said. He looked confused and it occurred to me the details of Bertie Schneider's death might not be exactly public. "Then let's just say that God wouldn't send anyone down from Heaven to say, 'Hey, the Cleveland Browns are going to win the Super Bowl this year.'" I forbore to say that might take divine intervention and nodded, seeing his point. He went on, "It's that finger on the scales thing, you know? When He intervenes that way, it's a very powerful thing, not to be wasted for minor stuff. So, if your apparitions consist of various holy figures chatting with you about who will win some TV game show, and you're not lying, it's preternatural, not supernatural. Or, of course, it's a diabolical deception. But those have their own ... characteristics. Which is what I wanted to talk about—"

Feeling sorry for Father Gnad's future parishioners and the future sermons they'd endure, I nodded again, and didn't speak, so as not to send him off down another track.

"So, diabolical deception, that is, the denizens from down below pretending to be heaven's emissaries, usually makes humans look silly or do unlikely stuff. One supposed Marian apparition, for instance, had the kids galloping backwards all over the landscape, and bending into weird shapes. That's in general not something that Heaven will do, because they respect human limits, and while they might increase them, they won't use their power to make you look ridiculous or demean you. Does that make sense?"

I thought of the various bands, singing about kittens and puppies, and of grown men decked in glitter and pink and started getting a really bad feeling.

"So, with that in mind, I want you to listen to this." He leaned forward and fiddled with the computer. Soon music emerged. It was heavy metal. I wouldn't call it Satanic metal. And it wasn't that bad, except for the lyrics which were the silliest I'd ever heard: "Fry my pork, Fry my pork, baby! Squeezin' my bacon so tight I'm a shakin'. Pretty baby!"

I opened my mouth to say something, but he stopped it. "Look, we were a little nuts. And kind of young. Yes, that was six months ago, but hey, I feel like it was decades. Besides, the drummer wrote the lyrics."

I didn't say a thing. Not a thing.

"Anyway, we were sitting around, and alcohol might or might not have been involved, and then suddenly we came up with the bright idea of playing the song backwards. It was silly, of course, and you know, people were joking about any Satanic messages you hear when playing a song backwards mean that you have to up your anti-psychotics, because, well, that's not how playing things backward works, and how would you manage to make it so that things played backward even had words, let alone coherent messages."

"Yeah," I said. "I've heard the arguments. And I never paid much attention. I think I'm too young to consider rock music satanic. Well, normal rock, you know?"

"Likely," he said. "Well, we were, too, which is part of the reason it was funny. We thought it was funny, at least." He took a deep breath. "And then we played it backward. And I have to tell you, I haven't listened to this backward since the first time, because ... well, you'll see."

He did something and music started playing. I expected the normal muddled sounds with about the same beat. Instead, bouncy music and pure sopranos came from the computer, "I love puppies, I love kittens, I love playing in the sun. Soap bubbles are so pretty. They make me feel nifty." He turned the thing off, and I noticed he shuddered and crossed himself.

"That can't be the same song," I said.

"That's what I thought, too. So I tried it with several other songs, and the result was normal. But put Fry My Pork in, and this is what you get."

I almost crossed myself, and would probably have done it if I remembered the right way to do it.

"So you think this is supernatural?" I said.

"No. Pretenatural. Or perhaps infranatural. I think this comes from the other side. Enemy action, as it were."

"Oh."

"Yeah. Oh. So the band disbanded and we … and I came back to my initial calling. I'm in a probation period, though they're allowing me to take some classes. I'd like to be less than fifty by the time I become a priest. Anyway … now you know. I don't know how much you're being paid to undertake this, nor why you're doing it, besides the payment, but I'm telling you, unless you have unshakeable faith, and a determination to … to take the enemy on, I'd stop. Stopping now is probably your best bet."

"But aren't we supposed to stop demonic attacks?"

He crossed himself again. "Listen, Mister Magis, the church has people trained to this. Special men. Men with broad backs and strong shoulders, who have unshakeable principles and keep themselves in a state of grace. The purpose of the enemy, the whole reason he exists, is to tempt the vulnerable. I don't think I could go toe to toe with him. I'm not that good. And I wouldn't advise anyone else to do it.

"I have no idea what is going on with this music thing, or why He has allowed it to go on, but I'm sure there is a reason and a purpose, and eventually someone stronger than I will step into the breach. But I'm not that guy." He folded his hands, one over the other. And I got a sense he was at peace, and where he belonged.

I was getting back into the Brown Disgrace when it occurred to me that was a pretty weird response for a future priest. Wasn't getting between Hell and whatever Hell wanted to do precisely the job of a priest? Look, I understand they're not all heroes, but they should at least be willing to have skin in the game.

And well, that was entirely his issue, right? Not mine. I had skin in the game. Or at least I thought so. If I failed at this, Rod would never give me another job, and money was tight enough as was. And then there was Emma. Okay, so Emma was not actually involved in this case. Probably. But if she heard I had stepped out of the way of pure evil? If she heard I had let other people suffer, while I was secure?

Emma appeared in my mind, straight as a pole, and full of … of some kind of pure purpose. Look, I probably didn't have a chance with her. That ship had likely sailed at least ten years ago. But I definitely wouldn't have a chance with her if she heard I had been afraid of some minor demon infestation, right?

5 PRETE INFRA SUPER... THIS STUFF JUST AIN'T NATURAL

THE THOUGHT HAD JUST GONE THROUGH MY MIND, as I drove through the blighted neighborhoods. It was that hour when the sun has mostly set, and the landscape was filled with crepuscular light, not quite there. This day was filled, too, with what I call "drowned light." It's hard to explain, but it's the sort of light you get some spring and fall days, when clouds obscure the sun just enough that it feels like you're seeing the entire landscape under water.

That's what it looked like, and it made the warehouses and surroundings even dingier.

The radio came on. Loudly. I jumped about a foot and almost drove off the road.

The radio hadn't worked in the Brown Disgrace since I'd got it. I'd tried it a number of times, to find it didn't work. If I really needed music – and normally only on very long drives – I listened to it on my phone, even if the speakers were tinny.

Now the radio came on, blaring loudly. It played Devil Inside by INXS.

I reached out and turned the radio off. I assumed that I'd hit a bump that had caused the car to make some kind of contact, and allowed the radio to come on. But I wanted to think. And I didn't want to go deaf.

The radio went off for like a second, then came on again, just as loudly, Words are weapons. Sharp as knives. Makes you wonder how the other half die. How the other half die. Makes you wonder, wonder, wonder–

Something on the rearview mirror caught my eye. It looked like, but wasn't quite, a coalescing cloud of ink-black dust. Look, you know those little tornadoes in Merry Melodies, the thing that appears when the Tasmanian devil spins? Yeah, something like that, inky black and swirling. And inside it

42

there was a suggestion of teeth and fangs and claws, something like, though not nearly as cute as, a spinning cartoon. More like the inside of the swirling cloud of dark was bigger than the outside, and also far spikier and full of pain. There were fangs and claws in that whirl, and a suggestion of sudden death and unquenchable hunger.

The Devil Inside was still blaring at top volume. I reached out, not even believing it would do anything and turned the volume down. I was right. It didn't do anything. At the same time I stomped on the accelerator to try to escape the cloud,

I avoided hitting a boarded up warehouse head on, went on the sidewalk for a block, twisted the wheel just before hitting a light pole, bounced onto the street, avoided an oncoming truck, the only other sign of life in this post-apocalyptic landscape, raced headlong down a pot-holed avenue. In the rearview mirror, doom chased closer and closer.

I was sweating, my hands slick on the wheel, like hands slipping on fresh blood.

I felt as if something were crawling down my back. Like a spider, if spiders were far scarier and had a lot more legs. The tornado of darkness was gaining on me. I remembered how Bertie Schneider had died, the eaten out place where his heart had been.

I didn't want to end that way.

"Now I lay me down to sleep, I pray the Lord my soul to keep." It was the only prayer I knew. It would have to do, though I'd never felt more awake in my life.

The radio was stuck. Or whatever was playing through it was stuck. It was all: The devil inside. The devil inside. Everyone of us the devil inside.

A man with dead eyes, dressed in tatters, came out of a darkened doorway and threw a bottle. I thought he was throwing it at the tornado of evil, but it hit the Brown Disgrace with a loud crash. Yeah, like the dent would even be noticeable.

The tornado swerved. There was a scream, a sense of whirling, as it enveloped the man, and then in place of the man there were clean bones, falling down in a glimmering pile.

"Now I lay me down to sleep. I pray the Lord my soul to keep." I turned down an alley, without thinking, trying to hide, trying to escape.

There was a brick wall, and no room to turn around. The tornado was six feet from the back bumper. "My soul to keep."

The phone rang, as I was looking around for a weapon. Any weapon. I had my gun in a shoulder holster, but I had an idea you couldn't shoot a demon. There was some cartoon character, when I was a kid, who'd killed one with a rocket launcher, but I couldn't remember which and at any rate, I was fresh out of rocket launchers.

I grabbed the phone blindly, with one hand. My other hand, in my pocket, found my mom's medal and I held onto it hard. So hard I could feel it imprint on my palm. I could hear my mother's voice, dimly remembered from childhood, saying the inscription on the medal, In Fatima, I prayed for you. It was better than nothing.

"Yeah?" I rasped into the phone.

The voice of the Priestling, Gnad, came on, "Mr. Magis? I had a sense I should call you."

"Uh … I'm kind of…."

Something hit the back bumper and made the car shake. It felt as if the car had been hit by an eighteen wheeler. I was sure I had a crunched area back there now, to match the massive dent in the front that had been there since I bought the car. The amazing thing would be if I still had a bumper.

I hadn't been particularly good, all things considered, but by and large I'd tried to help people and do the right thing. Surely I wasn't going to end this way, as a murder punchline. I clutched the medal so hard it would probably be imprinted in my hand forever. "I think there's a demon attacking my car. It's like … it's a tornado of darkness. It ate this guy, and it's—" Bang, smash. Something hit the bumper again. I was not looking at the back. I was not.

There was a sound like hands pounding on glass. I looked. I couldn't not look. Handprints formed on the glass, black handprints, as if of hands dipped in coal. All sizes and shapes, over and over again, till the back window was a blindness of soot.

"Magis, Magis," the voices said, high and insane. "Magis, let us in. Magis, Magis, Magis."

"That was my feeling," Gnad said, his voice preternaturally – was that the right word? – calm. "Look, quickly, it's not real."

I made a sound like laughing, only it wasn't real laughing, more what laughing would be if it were also a hiccup. "Was pretty real to the guy it ate." I regretted being in equal measures amused and horrified by Bertie Schneider's death. Dear Lord, they'd find me, with my heart eaten out.

"No, no, no. Listen. They don't have rights over you. You're an adopted son of God and baptized. You're human, anyway. They don't have power over humans. Unless the humans give them that power. Do you understand? You have to consent. You have to give them power. Half of the phenomena in the beginning of demonic attacks are to scare the person into giving consent. Into being so scared they let the devil in, they give it power over physical things and physical events." Did that mean that guy I'd watched be consumed had consented to being eaten? Who would consent to being eaten? You'd think you'd have to sign some form or something, and have it witnessed, perhaps notarized.

The radio blared louder than ever: The devil inside. The devil inside. Everyone of us the devil inside.

"Do you understand?" Gnad's voice was still perfectly clear, despite the radio.

I heard the something that was not a laugh escape through my lips again. "It's hard to through the—" Something slammed hard in the back again. And I realized something. Despite the crashes, the hard bangs against the car, the car hadn't budged. It hadn't budged an inch. The brick wall was still the same distance it had been.

It's not real, it's not physical. I pray to God my soul to keep.

There was a sound like an explosion.

The back window was clear. The soot was gone.

I was in an alleyway in a not so good part of town and felt suddenly very cool, as my sweat-soaked shirt clung to me. "Yeah," I said. "Yeah, I hear you. You..." My voice shook. "It seems we were right."

He sighed, a sound like a might gust. "God bless," he said as if it were a single word. "Stay safe."

That last seemed highly unlikely, since I'd never yet managed it in my life, but I was not about to dissuade him. The lights were just coming on, as the drowned light vanished. I backed the car out and headed home.

Before I could get there, the phone rang.

"Leb?"

It was Emma, and she was not well. Or at least she didn't sound well.

"What's wrong?"

"There's ... weird stuff happening. The house is shaking. Leb!"

"Scary stuff?" I said. "Supernatural stuff?"

"Y-yes."

"All right." I drove like crazy, first in the general direction of Dinkhelsbuhl, and then more specifically towards the streets I knew. "I'm coming. Remember this isn't real. I just learned that no matter how scary it looks and sounds, they can't actually touch you. These supernatural–" I stopped short. Damn Gnad, I now felt bad for using the wrong words, even though I had no idea what the right ones were, and had neither time nor expertise to repeat everything he'd told me at Emma. Not if she was under attack right now. "These supernatural things can't affect you physically unless you give them permission. Don't give them permission."

A nervous giggle came over the phone. "I'm certainly not giving any kind of affirmative consent!"

When I hit central Dinkhelsbuhl, the restaurants were hopping and the bars were starting to pick up. Did I mention the neighborhood had started going trendy?

The way these things happened, a lot of mom-and-pop restaurants and stores that served the neighborhood, had now become bars and restaurants, and one of the more misguided city councilmen had decided the new name for the area was "Dinkel." In the main street, where the drugstore and the candy shop used to be, they had a minor infestation of banners on the light poles. They flapped in the light breeze, proclaiming things like "Dinkel is for lovers" under a picture of a kissing couple, and "Dinkel is fun" under a picture of a full wine glass, because nothing says fun like wine. There was also "Art is Dinkel" with a picture of crossed, paint-laden paint brushes.

Judging from the crowd on that street, Dinkel was also loud, very young, and mildly annoying.

Stopping every few feet, to allow people to cross the street in front of me, I told Emma what the priest-trainee had told me over the phone, about how anything preternatural – or was it infranatural – couldn't attack anyone who didn't give them permission.

"I know," she said. And she didn't sound like she hadn't known before I told her, at that. "It's just Mom. She doesn't understand. She keeps trying to go there."

"Ooh, boy," I said. I didn't know where there was, but I was going to bet it wasn't good.

"I'm three blocks away," I said. "If the drunken students stop stepping in front of my car, I'll be right there."

By the time I started up the steps to Emma's place, I knew that something had gone very wrong in the house. I mean, they hadn't actually dented the Brown Disgrace. Or maybe they had. How would I be able to tell? But up on either side of the steps to the porch, plants were pulled up, and the earth below raw, as if someone had been digging in it.

And the next door neighbor was on her porch, looking like she wanted to say something. You know the look. Someone really wants to ask you something, but they either feel it's not their place, or they're afraid you'll think it's not their place.

She was a middle aged woman, in jeans and a plaid shirt, with her hair caught back in a ponytail. "Is everything all right in there?" she let out, as I rang the doorbell, sounding every bit like she didn't mean to say it, but it had just popped out. "Only it sounded like someone was torturing a cat."

"They don't have a cat," I said, just before Emma opened the door. The truth is, I didn't know if Emma had one or a dozen cats, but I was sure she wouldn't be torturing one. And how the hell do you tell the neighbors, They're just fighting a demonic infestation and I hope they're alright? All this non-natural stuff was horribly impolite, and I didn't know how to talk to anyone about it.

Then Emma opened the door. By the corner of my eye, I could see the woman turning away, as though embarrassed. And let me tell you right there, that this was not the stuff the old neighborhood had been made of. If the sounds coming from the house had been as weird as I expected, had it been in the old days, there would have been a circle of matrons around the front door, and a line after the circle, all demanding to know what was going on and insisting they be let in, to make sure everything was all right.

Everything wasn't all right. Emma looked like she'd been dragged through Hell by her heels. Her hair was up and pulled in all directions, like someone had raked it with claws. There were scratches on her face, one of which had broken the skin and was oozing droplets of blood. She was very pale.

"Oh, Leb," she said, and started to cry. There was relief, fear and grief, all mingled in her voice.

"What happened?" I said.

I didn't push her in the house, precisely, but herded her gently in, one arm not touching her but kind of surrounding her, and suggesting strongly she make her way inward. This wasn't the old neighborhood, and the last thing I wanted to do was cause the neighbors to be interested enough to do something stupid.

Something stupid in the old neighborhood had amounted to barging in, and, if needed, cleaning your house or spanking your kid. But I'd lived not too far from here the last ten years. The range of stupid in the twenty first century in this area of town was truly spectacular, and could range from a call to the police, on a suspicion of "someone with a gun" which would bring in armed Police in a mood to shoot dogs and make every inhabitant reach for the sky or else; to PETA picketing the house on suspicion of animal sacrifice.

Emma didn't resist my gestured suggestion, mind you, but went ahead of me into the house. The living room was turned upside down. Okay, only the furniture was. But that was spectacular enough, considering one of the pieces was a sofa that the Accorsos had had since I'd known them and which must have weighed about a million pounds, since it had never overturned when we were kids and jumping up and down on its arms.

The painting that hung over it was askew. The glass on the frame was broken.

Mrs. Accorso flapped around among the mess, like a cross between a helpless child and a disturbed bird. Her arms flapped, and she would try to turn something over or straighten it, while looking both bewildered and helpless. As I watched, she pulled the picture the other way, succeeding in skewing it in the other direction, and then sighed and walked around flapping her hands.

This was a relief, by the way. It meant she was still here. I had no idea what Emma meant by her trying to go somewhere, but I had a cold feeling in my stomach it would have been a bad, bad place.

"What happened?" I said. "Why are you crying?"

Emma rubbed at her face with her fingers, and then looked surprised at the blood on her right fingertips. "I'm sorry. I feel so stupid to cry. It's just–"

That was when Mrs. Accorso saw me. She fixed me with a clear gaze and said, "Magis? My daughter wouldn't let me go to that poor child. What is her name? Rose, Petal, Carnation … Lilly! She wouldn't let me go. And she had

47

this other child with her. They just wanted to play."

I looked at Emma. Her eyes widened.

"I'm sorry?" I told Emma. "Child?"

She made a face. "He had horns and a face … I can't describe it. They stood within a glow. He had pigtails. Red pigtails. In blue ribbons. Lilly said his name was Peggy. It was terrifying."

I felt a shiver go down my back and nodded.

"I'm sorry, Leb, I'm going to make a couple of phone calls. I'll be right back. Can you prevent Mom doing something stupid? Like leaving?" Emma asked.

I nodded again, as Emma walked into the house through the little hallway that led to her room, her parent's room, her mom's sewing room and the little room her father had used as an office. I wondered what it was now.

Things had fallen in place in my mind in a way I didn't like at all. I heard poor Bertie Schneider say, Call him Peggy, and a trickle of cold ran down my spine. It shouldn't be possible to be caught between horror and laughter, but I was. I wanted to laugh, cry and vomit, all at the same time. And I kept thinking, bizarrely, that devil in a blue dress was a thing, but devil in pigtails shouldn't be.

I'd just added one to one and gotten kumquat. That is, I'd just figured my two cases were related, and that whatever demonic influence was turning Satanic metal pink might be Emma's little missing girl.

Emma came back. She looked much happier, and had washed her face, or at least it was no longer bleeding. She'd also combed her hair.

"Lilly was in the middle of this demonic manifestation?" I asked her. Mrs. Accorso was in no way a reliable witness, of course. But she was an unsubornable one. Given where she lived, in some makeshift land of her decaying mind, what could anyone offer her to get her to lie?

Emma's eyes clouded again. She nodded, then went to the dining area, turned a chair over, and convinced her mom to sit in it. Then she started turning things right side up very carefully. I joined in. "Look," she said. "It's not something we can talk about right now. I called Mrs. Flores to come and look after Mom. Then we'll talk."

I helped her with the sofa. It weighed very little less than a million pounds, but between the two of us, we managed.

When everything was back in place, and we'd verified that the TV worked, Mrs. Flores was at the door, and Emma let her in. "Leb and I need to go out for a moment," she said. "Well, maybe a few hours. If you need anything, I have my cell phone."

From the sly look in Mike's wife's eyes, she thought that Emma and I were up to something and were getting away for a bit of hanky panky. I wished. I also realized, as she smiled at me, while Emma gave her a bunch of instructions, that she approved. That was probably why she'd come here at night, presumably leaving the kids with Mike. I'd found married women were not only unfathomable, they were also incorrigible match makers.

Emma collected her purse, headed down the steps, with me following. "Let's go in your car," she said, which tells you the level of her desperation. Because you know, no woman, ever, willingly asked me to go in the Brown Disgrace.

I waited till we got in to ask, "Where are we going?"

She waved her hand. "Actually we're only going two blocks away, but I want to talk. Can you go down Polk, very slowly?"

"Sure," I said. Since Polk was one of the president-named streets, it ran east-west. And two blocks would take us close to Main Street. Which meant that I had no option but to go slow, given the number of early-twenty-something people who thought they'd totally be immune to being hit by the Brown Disgrace.

As we crept west on the street, she said, "I know what a demonic manifestation is." And at my sideways look, she laughed, a sound like reluctance. "From reading, Leb. I didn't actually ever experience it. Not before this, at least."

"Why on Earth did you read about it?" She couldn't have been studying to be a priest. "Nunnery?"

She laughed again. "No. I studied psychology, remember? Or did you even know?"

I shook my head, because I really wasn't sure anyone had told me. I assumed she'd studied English or business, or something generic like that, because she hadn't been interested in the hard sciences. But that was all.

"Well, I did and one of the courses I took was about mental illness as perceived in the past. Weirdly, the professor wasn't an unbeliever nor did he scoff at people in the past. So he tried to explain he wasn't sure there wasn't such a thing as possession. He said that while there undoubtedly was a lot of attributing illness to the devil, you know like epilepsy and that stuff, he wasn't sure there weren't supernatural events that were known as such. As a result, I ended up reading up on everything from Marian apparitions, to stages of possession for a paper. So I knew what you were telling me about the weird, scary stuff. It's called Oppression, if I remember correctly. So I know a lot of that stuff, but this was weird. I mean, you don't expect this stuff in real life."

I told her about what had happened to me in the Brown Disgrace, then added, "The thing is that it's all weird. All of this. None of it should be possible or real."

"Well, yes. That I agree with. It's all very weird." She paused a second, then put her hand in front of her mouth, as if she wanted to prevent the next words coming out, then seemed to remove it by an effort of will and say, "I thought I was going mad, when there was Lilly there, next to this horrible thing in pig tails, and this other horrible thing that looked like a spikey basketball with too many eyes and fangs, saying 'Come on Emma. We'll play. We'll have so much fun.'"

"So she's dead," I said. And to my mind, honestly, it seemed weird because ... well, because little kids shouldn't go to Hell. Sure, okay, there are kids "tried as adults" for particularly heinous crimes, or kids that seem to be adults in everything but age. But everything I'd seen of Lilly and heard, too, even Emma's voice when she talked of the little girl, didn't make her sound like that kind of kid. More like a little imp yes, but imp in the sense we used it, of some kid who now and then got in trouble and did things wrong, but... oh, adorably wrong, not making the world a horrible place wrong.

"No," Emma said. It was singular and definite.

"What?"

"No. I think it's something ... I can't explain it, but I'm sure she's there physically. Not spiritually, as in dead, and that's where her soul went. I think that's part of what's wrong, at a guess."

I was quiet for a long while.

"Look, I know it sounds crazy, but she was more definite, she–"

"All of this sounds crazy, so what's a little more insanity between friends. But let's say she is in Hell physically," I said. "I was thinking maybe this was related to the bands going to the pink, but ... they've been doing that for two years, and she's only been missing for two weeks. Maybe Hell has gone crazy," I said. Which again, was weird. I mean.... Hell was supposed to be crazy, right, but not like making people sing about kittens and puppies and butterflies and wear pink crazy.pink. That was the sort of crazy that would only occur to a six year old girl. And it wasn't right. One liked to think of below and above as behaving in certain ways. If it all went crazy, then so would the Earth. I can't explain it, but it felt really wrong. Like, playing your Fry My Pork song backward and getting things about kittens and butterflies. Gnad was right. It was the sort of thing that scared you into the priesthood. And I didn't want to have to become a priest.

I gave Emma a sidelong glance. She looked beautiful, with her head slightly inclined and tilted to one side, as though she were thinking through something particularly difficult, and her mouth quirked, like something shouldn't be taken too seriously. There were slight creases at the corners of her eyes. Maybe they'd become wrinkles in time. She looked older than the last time I'd seen her, of course, but still just as gorgeous as she'd been in high school.

No, I didn't want to become a priest. Besides, they probably made you learn more than the one of two prayers I knew.

She sighed. "I don't know," she said, at last. "I don't ... it's nothing I can say and explain, and of course, everything is weird. But I thought we'd go and talk to Nancy. Nancy Edwards."

And to my blank expression, "Nancy Hathaway?"

I remembered, blurrily. Look, I'm not stupid, but I play stupid when Emma is around. Not on purpose, mind you. It's just, since kindergarten, everything disappears when Emma is around. But with effort, I could dredge up memories of a dark haired girl with a cutting sense of humor, and, usually, her head in a book. "She got married?" I said, surprised that she'd got her head out of her books long enough to notice men, much less marry one. Not to mention, she usually talked only about books and it scared even me, who was bookish and liked to learn.

"Yes. She lives on Madison," she said. We'd entered the part of town where every street was named for a president. It must have been fine when Dinkhelsbuhl was its own little town, and probably felt very proper and patriotic to people who'd newly come to America and were trying to show how American they were. It's like I swear half the old people in Dinkhelsbuhl when I was growing up were called America, or Liberty, or the name of some president, followed by some unpronounceable Eastern European name.

Now, it caused some problems, because of course there were other little towns now absorbed into Cleveland that had once had similarly bright ideas.

But in Dinkhelsbuhl I knew precisely where Madison was. I turned into it: a narrow street of tiny working man Victorians, two stories, small rooms, a lot, in fact, like Emma's place. Emma said, "Mrs. Minneti's old place."

And, of course, I knew exactly where that was. Mrs. Minneti had been a grandmother when we were kids. Meaning, she had grandkids, but not nearby. Both of her kids had moved somewhere. I no longer remembered where one had gone, but I remembered the one in California, because she used to show us pictures of her grandkids wearing shorts in winter. I remembered being jealous.

Thing was, her grandkids weren't here, obviously. So Mrs. Minneti, who must have been very lonely, would make cookies and stand on the porch of her house, spring, fall and even winter, if it wasn't blowing snow, waiting for school kids to pass by, like an amiable witch.

Amiable because she never tried to eat anyone. At least as far as I knew. Witch, because well ... what's the point of reference for someone who traps kids with sugary treats? Of course, all she wanted to do was give us cookies and milk or lemonade, and talk to us about her grandkids, and show us pictures.

Even as a little kid, I kind of understood how lonely she was, which is why I let myself be trapped so often. Well, that and because Emma seemed to go out of her way to get trapped. And I don't think it was for the cookies, because her mom made great cookies, too.

Anyway, we'd spent many happy hours in her little dark blue house with the weeping willow up front, because I was happy any place that had Emma, and Emma seemed happy listening to stories about these kids we'd never meet.

As I stopped in front of it, I realized the house was now pink. This wasn't even strange, since most of the neighborhood was all sorts of weird colors. People bought these dignified old Victorians and thought they were all so cute and precious that what they needed was to be bright yellow, or puce, or purple. At least it was a pretty salmon pink but … well … at this time and in this place, pink was getting a bad rep.

Emma seemed to read my mind. She chuckled. "Look, it's been pink for eight years. I don't think it's related to whatever this is. The people who bought it after Mrs. Minneti moved to a nursing home painted it this color before Nancy got it."

There were steps up to the yard, as there were in every home in the neighborhood, of course. Each side of the steps, instead of being lawn like the rest, was covered with what looked like wild roses. Hard to tell, but it crept, it was spikey and it had what looked like flowers on them.

"Why?" I asked. And because I was afraid she'd tell me why pink, I explained, "Why are we coming here?"

She shrugged. "Nancy collects oddities," she said. "Not things. Oh, that too. But mostly she collects people. I don't think she so much believes weird things herself, but she knows people who do. And for years now, she periodically mentions … strange creatures."

"What, like cryptids?"

She gave a weird sidelong glance. "No, like, Bigfoot. Or elves. Well, I guess they are cryptids, but that's not what I mean. I mean she looks at the world differently than us. She—" Emma shrugged. "She told me she thought that Lilly had got herself in trouble with something supernatural."

"Preternatural," I said, and got the weirdest look. "Right, never mind. Let's go talk to her. Maybe it will come to nothing, but if that really was Lilly and if she– Well!"

I had a sudden and uncomfortable feeling that the woman I loved was going to take me to Hell. And that it wouldn't be in the slightest bit metaphorical.

We rang Nancy's doorbell and she answered. Some people never get any different. They grow up, or even get old, but they look the same they did when they were young. Nancy had a couple of white hairs amid the black – Emma probably had white hairs, too, but it would be hard to see in the red – and also something that would one day be wrinkles around her eyes and on her forehead, like she'd raised her eyebrows one too many times. But she looked like the Nancy I'd known from high school, all grown up.

She smiled at me, but gave me no extravagant greeting. We'd probably seen each other around now and then, right? After all I didn't live that far away. But I'd never seen Emma. Dinkhelsbuhl was its own world. If you didn't shop the local stores and go to local events, you might as well live across the world.

"Come in," she said. "And don't let the idiots out."

I had no idea who the idiots were, and it seemed like a weird way to refer to kids – though not necessarily wrong; hey, I remember being little – but when we got into the hallway, I felt something rub around my ankles, and realized it must be cats. Or dogs. But it felt like a cat.

It was dim in the little hall, but I could read a sign on the wall that said, "Don't let the cats out, no matter what they tell you."

From the hall to the living room, and I figured the furniture in the house was eclectic. Yep. Eclectic. Which means it was odd, and had no particular unifying style, but not weird. And certainly not expensive enough to be eccentric.

The sofas were just sofas, but the table in between them was a tree trunk cut to size, with a glass top on it. I could see – without stopping to look – interesting artifacts along the walls, bowls and sculptures and stuff. And there were cats. One, a black and white one, with a patch of white over the right eye, giving him the impression of saying "really?" at anything you said, opened one eye to me. I petted him. Because one does, when coming near cats. Or if one doesn't, the cat lets us know we've transgressed horribly. Cats. They're all ambassadors from some terribly formal culture.

Nancy went off to the kitchen and we followed. For a minute I thought that she had acquired Mrs. Minneti's cookie-making obsession with the house, but the kitchen smelled of fresh baked bread, not cookies, and Nancy was gesturing at the kitchen table. "There's tea and coffee," she said. "Help yourselves."

There was coffee, and the cups were hanging under the upper cabinets. I grabbed one, helped myself to coffee, and sweetened it from the sugar bowl, then sat down. Nancy looked at my mug, "People give me these mugs, so I use them. But that one is all wrong. They're not, you know. They're more like little aliens in fur suits. That's why I like them."

I looked at the mug. It said, "Cats are like kids in fur suits."

Emma's, which she filled with boiling water from the stove, and dropped a tea bag into, said, "Friends are the family we choose." Nancy didn't seem to have a quibble with that saying. She sat, tucking her feet in so they disappeared in the folds of a colorful velvet skirt. "It's about the girl, isn't it? What's her name? Aster ... no, Lilly." She looked towards me and said, "I don't particularly like kids. I don't dislike them, mind you, but I wouldn't go out of my way to interact with them. But I noticed the kid, Lilly, sometime ago. She's a bit like a cat. Self-contained and ... strange. Different in herself. Emma, of course, likes her, but Emma likes most kids, even the awful ones." Something of teasing in her eyes gave me the impression this was a conversation the two friends had often had before. "The thing is," she said, "since I noticed Lilly we've talked about her a lot. And since she's been missing, I've had the impression she's gone ... sideways. Elsewhere."

I looked at her, not sure what to even ask. If I opened my mouth, it would be super, infra, and peter confusing for everyone.

Nancy smiled as if she got what I didn't say. "Look, most adults forget this stuff when they get older, but kids have really weird experiences," she said. "I know I did, and if you cast your mind back, you'll probably remember weird experiences you had. I mean, if you're willing to remember it. Reality is not as ... fixed for kids. I remember stepping sideways, as it were, and out of reality into other realities where things were different. Don't you?"

What I remember was Nancy not being this weird. That was my first thought. But then I saw Emma looking at me very seriously, as though willing me to think and believe. And we'd agreed that all of this was very weird, but was still happening despite our certainty that it shouldn't be. And yes, okay, there were some weird memories, all the way back there. Things about glowing walls, and I had a weird memory of something like a cat, but with purple antennae, stuff way back before my parents died. "I always assumed that was just my imagination."

"People do, of course," Nancy said. And it was like she was telling us that of course people sometimes caught colds. "I mean, once we know more about the world and we know some things are impossible, we stop remembering those things as real, and start saying things about kids being so imaginative. But if you're broken in a particular way, you remember it for a long time, and you know it's true. Or it was true." She had made herself tea, and now wrapped both hands around it. A little calico cat jumped on her lap. "I remember. And I could see from Lilly's behaviors what she was up to. And then she got interested in all the wrong stuff."

I raised eyebrows. I can't begin to tell you all the things that went through my head when people said that kids got interested in wrong stuff. I'm a PI. I've found a couple of little bodies in a ditch, and heard about a lot more found in other ditches.

"New Age," Emma said. "She means New Age."

"Most of which is nonsense, like most mystical stuff," Nancy said. "Thing is, sometimes the nonsense is dangerous. And kids don't know the difference between dangerous and cool. I have a dragon on my mailbox, so the kids kept asking me all sorts of weird things."

"A dra—"

"Look, people have cardinals and stuff painted on their mailboxes. So one day I went nuts, went outside, got hold of the mailbox, brought it in, and painted a dragon on it. This stuff is useful. If the neighbors get to thinking, Ah, Nancy, nice young lady, the dragon keeps them from getting really friendly. A cat would have done as well, but it wouldn't be as much of deterrent. As is, most people think I'm weird and leave me alone. Some guy down the street, whose sense of science fiction and fantasy must have been ablated at birth, came by and tried to exorcise me. And, of course, I get the occasional teen who wants me to teach him about Satanism."

"To teach them about what?" I asked.

She grinned. "Oh, one of them wanted me to teach him how to become possessed."

I choked on my coffee and Emma had to slap me on the back.

Nancy looked amused. "It's not real, you know? Most of them are just raised with the idea only the material exists. So when they even hear of witchcraft or whatever, the first time, they just think it's cool. It's a new thing. They have no concept of evil. Not real evil. So, they walk around asking and wishing for stupid things."

She snorted. "Which frankly is also good but in another way, because it gives me the chance to tell their parents that their kid is either crazy or has moved from pot to the hard stuff. So, goodness all around. But this girl, Lilly, would come by and ask me about the habits of dragons and what they ate. I fed her a couple of Pern books, of course, and the Wizard of Earthsea, and Tolkien, but she said she sometimes talked to them, and then things went weird.

"When she disappeared I wondered if she hadn't gone some place weird, if she hadn't stepped sideways away from reality. You see, Emma had told me about a creature in a suit with a head of a mean dolphin that Lilly said was hiding in her closet. Seemed like a demon of some sort to me."

Emma set her cup down, hard. "I did, didn't I? I didn't even remember that. I thought it was just a bad dream."

"Right," Nancy said. "But I had my suspicions. And then I heard about the Satanic bands, and pink and stuff. And that some guy named Albert Schneider had got killed in a horrible way."

She shrugged. "I'm not religious. It's not that I'm atheist, I never spent that much time thinking about it that I can deny believing with any certainty. It's more that I don't care. My family didn't care. I was never really interested. So I don't know about all this satanic stuff, but … it's possible that's what the kid got into. Look, I never had kids. But Lilly's parents are worse than that. They also have no interest in children, but they had her, and they treat her kind of like a knick-knack. They show her off and that's it.

"Children who don't fit in, particularly smart ones, can find their way to some really strange reading stuff. And heck, half of our television series don't get the difference between genuinely evil and just weird. We started that confusion with Japanese cartoons, I think, because they don't get Western concepts."

My mind reeled. This woman talked very fast and covered territory I was not used to even thinking about. But in the bind we were in, I had to think about these uncomfortable topics, right? No matter how much I disliked to.

I cleared my throat, "So, you're saying?"

"Are you saying that Lilly went to Hell? Literally? Physically?" Emma asked. "Seems ... weird. But, with the pink and the bands, well, stuff has happened. Leb has been working on that case...."

Slowly, reluctantly, I told Nancy the story of what had happened with Rando and his investigation. She frowned through it, and afterwards got up to get herself some tea. She came back, put honey in her tea, and stirred it. "You know," she said. "You act like all of this is so bizarre, but it is obvious this is what happened. It sounds to me, guys, like a six year old girl has taken over Hell. I don't know how that can happen, but the obsession with pink alone indicates it. That and the complete lack of understanding of a will other than her own."

"But," I said. "Lilly has only been missing two weeks. This stuff with the bands started two years ago."

She shrugged. "Look, I don't know how much of the stuff we think we know about the supernatural, or whatever is true, and how much just what our ancestors felt like writing, but everyone agrees when you cross over, be it to Hell or fairyland or whatever, time changes." She paused and sipped her tea, and suddenly her eyes danced with amusement. "Of course, it might be just a plot device to make stories more interesting."

And it could be, but yeah, she had a point. I remembered my teen years and reading some very weird things that agreed with that time-slip thing.

"The thing is," Emma said, "how could a six year old take over Hell? And more importantly, how do we get her back? Because if we don't, sooner or later she's going to get at least Mom to cross over. She appeared to us, and tried to ... convince us to come to where she is." Emma shuddered and told the story. Nancy's eyes grew wide at the description of Peggy. "Mom doesn't get it, and it's all...." She made a helpless gesture.

For the first time, in her expression, I caught a glimpse of the burden Emma had been carrying, and how much her mom's deterioration had eaten her life. How she felt responsible for her mother as one would feel responsible for a child or a pet, and unable to see a way out of it or any way it even got better at all. Just able to keep the person going. Often alone. Often ignored. Not able to talk to anyone about how difficult her life really was.

How many people lived like this, taking a thankless task over, without complaining, without the people around them being aware of the immensity of the undertaking? Maybe that's why she looked after Lilly and the other kids. At least there was hope for them. They were growing and improving and someday they'd be on their own.

Nancy looked thoughtful. "There's this guy," she said. "He'd be pagan if, you know, he believed enough to be pagan and if he weren't essentially a scientist. He's been involved with this group that studies the supernatural from a ... scientific perspective. Little known, but.... Okay, the Soviets studied this stuff, and we did too, back from the seventies on. But all the results seemed to suffer from irreproducibility. It's not that they can't be reproduced. It's that the way they're reproduced is not ... predictable. Which invalidates the very idea of studying this. The Soviets eventually fell, and we supposedly gave this stuff up, but not really. There is just enough there to get DARPA grants, and keep this stuff going. It's just that it's all...." She made a gesture like trying to grab something midair, that somehow transmitted the idea of something disintegrating as it was touched. "But I'm friends with him. He's interesting. He runs a small lab nearby. I have no clue if he has answers to how this kid got there, or how you can get her to come back. Or even if that was what had happened. But I can put you in touch with him. If you want. I just thought of it because we sometimes have coffee in the morning, and he told me there's something really weird going on with polarity, or something."

"We could go back to almost-Father-Gnad," I said, hesitantly, thinking his phone call had saved my bacon, back there. "Maybe he knows how we can go to Hell and save Lilly."

"My guess," Emma started, putting her hand over mine on the table. Her fingers felt very cool and firm. "Is that he'd disapprove of anyone trying to go bodily to Hell. And he'd probably say Lilly couldn't be there. Maybe not, but.... My family was more religious, remember? And Mom would have said that stuff like that was possible, maybe, but the priests...." She made a face. "I get the strong feeling that most Catholic priests have stopped believing in the supernatural. I could be doing them an injustice, mind you. It's entirely possible they're just trying to keep people off the dangerous stuff."

I frowned. "That latter is the feeling I got. But yeah, he probably wouldn't approve of us doing anything with it. After all his job is to keep people from going to Hell, isn't it? Mind you, I'm not sure about rescuing her? I'm not sure it's possible. If she's there, which seems impossible."

Nancy made a sort of sigh-huff and muttered something about believing impossible things sometimes being the only sane thing to do, then said, "So, do I call him or not?"

We sort of nodded. I felt like I'd fallen down a rabbit hole of weird, but with Emma's hand on mine, I was willing to take a lot of weird and not complain.

"Okay, I'll call Odell then."

6 ODD

IT TOOK HER FIFTEEN MINUTES ON THE PHONE. Not to talk to this man, but to get hold of him. It was after work hours, so Nancy called his cell phone and got nothing, called a phone number that was his wife or girlfriend – judging from the sounds coming over the phone and the lively discussion of, "Where has Odell got to now?" The conversation veered into something wrong with the cat, Tesla, and from that to … something else, and finally Nancy was given the phone number of Jolie LaChance who, "Should be at the lab with him." That number once called got the phone handed to Odell, who apparently had forgotten to charge his phone, but was really interested in our story, in outline, and told us to, "Come along to the lab."

He met us at the lobby of one of the not terribly expensive high-rises at the edge of the gentrified area. From décor and the general feeling of not being particularly well kept up, it was obvious this multi-story building just outside Dinkhelsbuhl proper had gone up in the eighties, in the expectation of great amounts of business before Cleveland, like all the post-industrial midwest had migrated *en masse* south and west, leaving these buildings untenanted or cheap. Or both. From the sign up front, with a bunch of "names" missing from the large board indicating the tenants, it was obvious a lot of people had moved out, and others moved in who did not advertise their presence.

Though to be fair Dr. Odell Brant did advertise. Or at least his organization, Infinite Mind, did. Of course, by that name it could be anything from a puzzle company to a testing service.

What it was might have been something between those.

Dr. Brant met us in the lobby, which was mostly deserted. He was a middle aged man, at that undefinable age between 40 and 60 that some men hit. Lived in, but not old. Spare to the point of extreme thinness, he had reddish hair that had faded to blond, or blond hair with a hint of red, a lot of it, and it stood up in all directions in the ever popular Einstein look, except he kept it clipped to about two inches of length. His ears stuck out of the fuzz, his nose was tall and thin, and he wore oversized glasses. His jeans and grey T-shirt seemed oversized too. He'd have looked like a cartoon character, except that his blue eyes behind his oversized lenses looked very serious, very attentive, and incredibly intelligent.

He wore a massive badge on a lanyard, and shook our hands firmly, in turn. "Odell," he said, when we addressed him as Dr. Brant. "Or Odd. My wife often calls me Odd. So does Jolie, my assistant. Come on. Let me take you up to where we can talk. What Nancy said made it sound like you have the solution to something that's been bothering me for a couple of years."

He led us to an elevator, which to my surprise, had a proximity sensor for the badge. He waved his badge near the sensor, then pressed the 10th floor. "You can't go up without one of these. It's not ... well. What we're doing is secret, I suppose, but only in the sense that DARPA asks for certain rules of secrecy, you know, since this is supposed to be defense work. But frankly we also prefer some isolation. The two floors beneath us are empty. We'll move if someone moves in. What we've found is that when we are doing experiments that involve ... well, not to get into specialized terms, that which can't quite be seen and perceived by senses or instruments, it helps to keep ... other influences away, if you want the results to be consistent."

"We'll go to my office. We have certain things that insulate it from the test area proper. I'll give you a tour once some experiments have run."

We came out of the elevator into an atrium with a very fake potted tree and two chairs on a table between the chairs was a pile of leaflets. Walking by, I read – upside down – the massive header: *Are you psychic?*

I had a vague memory of seeing a stack of those to the entrance of a local diner.

There were more of them, as well as a stack of leaflets headed *Test your precog* sitting on Dr. Brant's desk. As well as piles of folders, a few notebooks, a book called Voices in the Storm, with a bunch of little colored sticky markers, and a coffee mug with, "What are the facts?" on it.

He smiled hazily at us, and said, "Coffee?"

We accepted. In my case, mostly for the sake of having something to hold onto. It's easier to tell a weird story – like the one about the bands – if I have something to fiddle with. I had a feeling before this night was done, I was going to be sloshing with various kinds of caffeine. Or not. Was there caffeine in Hell? More importantly, were there restroom facilities?

He left and came back a few moments later with two mugs. Emma's said, "I know what you're thinking," and mine said, "Sensor," and I refused to even guess the context under which someone had that stuff put on mugs.

"Okay, so, tell me what the problem is. Nancy said some things that don't make sense in context."

For the third time, I told the story of Rod Rando's problem. To Dr. Brant's credit, he only giggled a little at the description of the hard rock bands, some – though not all – with Satanic overtones going be-pinked and singing about puppies and kittens. If his lips twitched at the description of butterfly clips on moustaches, it was all gone by the time I described Bertie Schneider's murder. And he looked somewhat confused by "Peggy" and perhaps mildly horrified. He nodded through the description of Brian Lee Gnad's explanation of the various realms, and seemed like he was going to say something when I described the attack of the murderous tornado, but then said, "I'll talk at the end."

He then turned to Emma, "So," he said. "What happened on your end? Nancy said something about a little girl in Hell."

He listened gravely while Emma talked of Lilly. He looked up the website her parents had made for her and frowned at it. His brow creased as Emma described the attack on her house and the vision of Lilly.

His lips quirked, and he rotated a pen in his hand. At the end, he called Nancy and asked her what she knew of Lilly, and listened, while making a few notes.

After a while, he hung up, and went off, in obvious search of coffee, without offering more. Mind you, I wasn't done with my coffee, though it had gone stone-cold.

Which was okay. I just wanted to hold it.

He sat down. "Okay, what your friend, the priest—"

"I don't think he's a priest yet," I said. "More like a priest larva, and besides, I'm not sure he's my friend. I barely talked to him."

"Okay, what your acquaintance the seminarian said is broadly true. There seem to be several realms that are circumscribed in what is broadly known as 'supernatural' in common parlance. Most of the ones I think are understandable and … *explorable*, because they don't require us to take a religious position – and understand here I'm constrained by government funding which is definitely not religious – is the preternatural realm, which includes most of what we'd call 'refugees from fantasy' as well as possibly all the classical gods and such. I know some traditions hold them to be demons, but it's entirely possible they're just intelligent creatures playing in different realms and with different forces, who chose to pretend to be divinities. Or perhaps didn't pretend at all, but humans assumed so. It's hard to tell, because we lack a non-religious vocabulary to talk about it. We broadly speaking stay out of supernatural and infranatural realms. Except…."

"Except?" Emma prompted.

"Except that we seem to have no choice in this, lately. Most of the experiments we do here are the standard ones, with the addition of some magnetism and electricity stuff. Anyway, most of what we do is the old, visualize cards and tell what the other person is looking at, with simple decks, or precognition of what will come next, though we've also played a bit with astral projection. Our current projects involve far viewing and influencing. I can't explain closer than that, unless you're cleared. But—" He shook his head. "Lately, for about two years, we've been getting what can only be called a series of SOSs from Hell."

"Pardon?" I said. I mean, if there was a Hell, I'd expect the SOSs would be more or less continuous. After all the theme song of Hell should be, *We've Got to Get Out of This Place*, right?

"Oh, and commands from Heaven. We've been getting in no uncertain terms that there is something very wrong. That through a ... well, probably through a very bad act on someone's part – like a demon's, and yes, demons can have bad acts for them, when they jeopardize the structure they depend on – a child was traded into Hell.

"And this ties in with our institute in a way. You see, last month we hired this college kid, Curtis Ackerman. We didn't know he'd been reading a lot of weird New Age books. Normally we screen for the most dangerous ones in our entrance interview, but we were hiring a lot of people at once, so we didn't." He ran his hand through his hair, paradoxically enhancing the Einsteiness of it. "He thought he could capture a demon and prove once and for all that all of this exists and become famous, or increase our funding or whatever. Except that's not how any of this works."

Dr. Oddell sighed. "Anyway, he came to us and said he'd made a summoning circle and something came through, but whatever it was had escaped him. Security tapes showed a creature with the head of a shark or I suppose a mean dolphin... like what you describe in the little girl's closet. We fired Curtis but it's obvious to me what came through was some minor minion from the infranatural regions, and he somehow tried to take a hostage, perhaps to be allowed back, in the principle of innocent sacrifice and all that."

He made a face. "But that was a problem, because the child is there bodily, which means she has powers and gifts that exceed what anyone there has. And also, because she was, apparently – and that would be the severe error – a true innocent, with an inner sense of right and wrong. Possibly acquired from you, Emma. Which in turns causes ... problems. These have somehow enabled her to take over, causing a serious disruption of the balance, because she's not the thing of evil that anchors that pole. And that disruption in turn is disrupting everything."

His eyes shining, he straightened up. "Imagine Heaven, Hell and Earth, oh, and the preternatural, which would be a realm parallel to Earth, as ... vibration frequencies. They all exist at the same time in the same place. There are things humans can do to bring themselves to another frequency. For the supernatural and infranatural realms, that has to do with acts of great sanctity or acts of great sin, though we've managed to fake it for the infranatural ... or at least we have some idea how to do it. For the preternatural realm, it is again different, and the ones who most often cross over seem to be artists or children. We've managed to achieve that fairly regularly."

"I'm sorry, you've sent people to fairyland?" Emma asked.

He waggled his hand. "Yes, but transitorily. More like we tracked such denizens in this land that have crossed over from fairyland, and – say, you say you're a PI?" he asked me.

When I nodded, he said, "We might have reason to talk to you. Not directly related to our current projects, but what an impact that could have. Anyway, I was talking about the disruption of having someone in charge of Hell, whose vibrational frequency is all wrong. You have to understand that it's changing things. Oh, it won't for long. What she's doing, because her underlings only know one way to accomplish things, will change her to their vibrational frequency. Very soon, she'll become the role she's playing. That's how these things work. She'll be taken over, transformed. And cease to be a corporeal entity."

"You're saying she'll die!" Emma had gone pale.

"Well, yes. That's one way to put it. The thing is that though technically that has to happen very fast, because no human can survive Hell that long, because of the differential in the passage of time, the repercussions on this side could take forever to play out, and while they do we'll be in jeopardy and confusion." I realized he was mostly concerned by what Lilly's death, or transformation in Hell, would do to other places in reality, not for Lilly, and I liked doctor Brant a little less. But then he hesitated and said, "Nancy said you wanted to go to Hell?"

Emma nodded, "And bring Lilly back, yes. Is it possible?"

Dr. Brant took a deep breath. "Oh, it's possible. I'm just not sure it's ... advisable."

"What does that mean?" I asked.

"Well, you guys should be aware that though we've sent people to Hell a couple ... a couple of times, and other people did before us – in the seventies, the Soviets thought it might be a way to cross over undetected to the US – only one person has survived. He was and is extremely devout. He went through, but not unchanged, and in fact when he came back he left research, and converted to one of the more fundamentalist religions. He's not very well known yet, but I suspect one day he'll be. He went over as a member of a party of twenty, and he says only he survived, because he's the only one whose faith carried him through and made him impervious to attack."

"But you said that being corporeal in Hell is a very powerful thing."

"Sure, but only if you can avoid either being driven mad or becoming lost. And that only seems to be possible if something like either faith or utter innocence protects you. The Soviets attempted corporeal journeys and none of their people survived."

"Oh. But can you do it for us? Anyway?" I asked. Suddenly I had this strong feeling that if we were going to pull the kid out, we needed to be as corporeal, as solid as she was. "Can you send us there physically?"

"I think so. It is ... vibrational frequency. And I think ... I think we can make it so you get there. I'm just not sure we can bring you back, or keep the way open so you come back. We know this is possible, because there is a long tradition of people making the journey and coming back. Now, most of those from the ancient world sound like hallucinatory trips, but we also have testimony from Orpheus and Eurydice and ... there is a possibility that you can indeed go in physically, and come back physically. Maybe. I want you to understand that the overwhelming chance is that you, too, will change. You'll have to make compromises. You'll have to taint yourselves to survive. And if you do that, then you won't be able to come back. Do you understand?"

I understood. And I didn't like it even a little bit.

I could tell by Emma's face she didn't either. I heard her say something under her breath that sounded like, "If only Mom...."

Followed by "But then Mom probably won't survive another attack like what we had."

She took a deep breath and squared her shoulders. "I have to go. I have to get her back. I'm sorry. I raised that kid practically from kindergarten. What Nancy said was true. Her parents ignored her, at least since she was old enough to feed and clean herself, which is when they let her nanny go. Without me, she'd be a different kid. In a way, she's my kid. My responsibility. And I must go get her." She turned to me, very serious, very pale, but with a smile, as though she'd pasted the expression on and was forcing it. "Leb, if everything goes wrong, I need someone to take care of Mom. I know it's an awful lot to ask, but she knows you and ... honestly, you can probably sell the house, and take over the estate. Just put her somewhere nice. Most of the time, she can't remember where she is or what she's doing, but she is still a very nice person."

I heard the words come out of my lips before I knew what I was going to say, "I can't look after her," I said. "I'm going with you."

Tell me what sense that made. Look, I wasn't even sure any of this was true. Maybe there had been no demonic attack when I was in the Brown Disgrace. Maybe I hallucinated it all. I mean, I practically hadn't slept since this began, and if we're going to talk about the way I habitually ate, well ... there could be some buildup of convenience store tacos and hotdogs that induced hallucination, right? Not to mention the Slim Jims I consumed in mass quantities while out and about on investigations.

But here I was ready to go to Hell for a little girl I hadn't even met. Oh, and I guess to solve Rod Rando's problem, too, but that was secondary. I mean, there had to be better ways of earning a living than going to Hell, right? I heard the local supermarket was hiring....

"Leb," Emma said, mildly chiding, as if she saw everything I'd thought, and agreed that going to Hell was a stupid thing for me to do, and thought that maybe, just maybe, I'd lost my mind.

"No," I said, answering the question she hadn't asked. I was ninety nine percent sure I wasn't possessed, or crazy, but something had control of me, and the something that was in charge had zero percent to do with my rational self. "No, it's no use chiding me. I'm going with you. There's no way I'm going to let you take care of this on your own."

"But Mom–"

"If you're willing to sign documents to let me make decisions about the estate and your mom's care, you can trust someone else. Like ... maybe Nancy?"

Her face lit up. "She'll hate me," she said. "But Nancy would do well by Mom, I think. At least in terms of finding someone to look after her. She's not cruel. And anyway, she'll feel responsible, which is the important thing."

Minutes later it was all under way. A call to Nancy took care of the problems with Mrs. Accorso's care. And Dr. Brant called people – at what was nearing midnight – to come draft the documents and witness Emma's signature. He also called some people to come back to the lab. And he got them in. I was starting to wonder how much he paid. Okay, it sounded like a loony place to work in, but it wasn't like most of my work was sane, anyway. And it was probably better than supermarket cashier.

Part of the issue was how to get to Hell. Hold the jokes. Yes, I know – I know – it's supposedly easy and well paved and a lot of people skate into Hell without noticing. Also making inappropriate jokes too soon after a disaster is said to send you to Hell.

But this was more literal. Apparently we could walk to hell, with backpacks, but I was against. There was some talk about getting us a van or a bus.

Dr. Brant called on the police to close some streets – how much power did he have? – and evacuate any buildings that still had people in them, in this industrial/business area in the middle of the night. Which wasn't many, frankly.

And I started to get scared. I never thought I'd go to Hell. Not physically.

7 Disgrace in Hell

I KEPT WANTING TO ASK IF WE SHOULD PACK A TOOTHBRUSH, but that seemed like the sort of thing one didn't ask on the eve of this kind of project. Emma, meanwhile, went about it as if she were planning a camping trip.

It made me imagine what she would be like if we had got married out of high school: planning trips with our six kids, running an efficient household....

Dr. Brant's assistant or whatever – he just called her his right hand – was a slim blonde woman with intelligent eyes. Dr. Jolie LaChance somehow made, "Just call me Jolie," easier than Dr. Brandt did.

She had a clipboard and a brisk manner and she came on the scene to get us ready for our trip. From that moment on, it became hers and Emma's show.

You see, unlike me, Emma had no problems asking if we'd need toothbrushes in Hell.

Jolie made a face. "Probably not," she said. "Look, if you end up there for more than a day, subjective, from your point of view you're going to be in a world of trouble, and none of it will involve the danger of cavities.

"Your first problem is that time runs differently in Hell. Well, to be fair, it runs differently in all planes of reality. We have legends about a second in Heaven being like a million years on the Earth, and everyone knows of things like Rip Van Winkle and people who cross into fairyland coming back either to find they'd lived for years there but only minutes had passed on Earth or that conversely they'd been there for ten minutes but a hundred years had passed on Earth and everyone they knew was dead.

"Hell is yet worse than fairyland for that. Time seems to run irregularly in currents and it makes no sense whatsoever, has no connection whatsoever to our world or our time. In fairyland time still goes forward, just at different rates. In Hell it runs backwards, forwards, and possibly yes. You might find yourself pushed forward and backward at once. So, if you come out, you sometimes find you traveled in time backwards.

"One of the guys we thought we were sending to fairyland ended up in Hell. He got out but somehow ended up in the nineteenth century. We know because he left a letter to be delivered to us. He seems to have had a decent life, but he was nowhere near us in time. So time travel backwards is in the realm of possible."

Emma looked mulish. "I think the nineteenth century would still be better for Lilly than Hell."

"Sure," Jolie shrugged. "Anyway what I meant is that your chances of succeeding are close to zero, but even if you do, the chances of coming back to our time with the kid are even slimmer. Never mind toothbrushes. It all gets worse the more time you spend on that side, because Hell is chaos and staying there gives more chances for chaos to take effect. Does that make sense?"

"Clear as mud," I said, and she smiled at me, a tight smile. But Emma said, her voice matter of fact, "So, what can we take with us that will increase our chances of coming back?"

I heard myself blur out, "Can we take my car?"

Okay, okay, it as probably a subconscious desire to destroy the Brown Disgrace. Look, most of the time it was a zombie car, alive by unnatural forces, so it would seem a given.

Perhaps part of me wanted the Disgrace to die already, so I could buy another car. Any other car at all. After all, it did guzzle gas, and with it my scant and irregular paychecks.

"It's cheaper than a van. If I lost it, I would only be out $700."

Jolie looked puzzled. "Beg your pardon?"

"Good idea," Emma said. "Will that help or hurt?"

"Most cars its age are dead," I quipped, but it only got me a quelling look from both women. Humor is a place where the sexes rarely meet.

"We don't know," Jolie said. "Our guys before didn't take a car. But we can't say their experience was a rousing success either."

"So, can we take guns?" Emma asked, and before Jolie could recover. "Oxygen tanks? Thermal Suits? Buckets of holy water? What will increase our chances of returning? Do you have any data on any of that?"

Jolie raised her eyebrows, mumbled, "Just a moment." She left the room and came back with Doctor Oddell. "Very interesting idea," he told Emma. His eyes sparkled. "If you want to approach this as a voyage of exploration into hostile territory … well, that is something we never thought of doing."

"But it is what Hell is, isn't it?" Emma asked. "Hostile territory. Particularly if we want to bring Lilly back out."

"Yes, yes," Dr. Oddell said. "I'm not saying you are wrong. Rather that we've never done it." He tilted his head to the side looking bird-like. "I suppose it's logical, but most of the other people we sent through were not ... you know, they were going in merely in a spirit of scientific enquiry."

"So did a lot of the 19th century explorers," Emma said. "But they went armed. And often brought back stuffed and mounted specimens, not that this is what we intend to do."

"Oh, yes, undoubtedly." He smiled, and Jolie behind him looked interested. "So what did you have in mind? Jolie said something about firearms but I'm not sure that's your best bet since those might or might not work, but more importantly, in some of the variable environments in Hell they might act as bombs and blow you and the car up. That's just from probes we've sent for measurements. Totally different physics. So taking guns might be counterproductive."

"That's ... good to know," Emma said. "Should we sit down and make a list, so that we know everything you've tried that might be dangerous?"

In the end it was decided we would in fact take the Brown Disgrace. This made more sense if you understand that in addition to the sin load or whatever – making the car into a scape-car, I guess – I tell you that the rest of the list of things to take occupied several pages. There was no way we could hump all that equipment on our backs.

I'm not sure, supposing I ever remembered, what the entire list of every single thing we took was. Let's just say that the back of the Disgrace was packed.

The back seats were left free because, as Dr. Oddell said, "We're allowed to hope maybe you'll come across one or two of our lost researchers, yes? And perhaps you can give them a ride back."

For some reason, the idea of picking up hitchhikers in Hell seemed seriously inadvisable, but when you're already doing something incredibly dangerous, to pile on more danger doesn't seem particularly weird.

So, as I remember, we took two spare cans, ten gallons each of gas, just in case the engine continued to work in Hell – some experiments indicated it was possible – and we had to drive so far we ran out of gas. Which to be fair, in the Disgrace, was no more than about fifty miles.

Then there was food.

Question: Why does a psychic research center store MREs?

Answer: I don't know. I just know they did, and that a lot of my veteran friends would say the MREs deserved to be in Hell.

Other random things that got piled in the back included a half a dozen stainless steel baseball bats – apparently made to order. "An experiment," Dr. Odell said, and then significantly, "Fairyland." – all blessed by a local priest who seemed neither surprised nor disturbed at being called in in the middle of the night. Perhaps they had him on retainer. I really wanted to know more of what these people did.

He also blessed a couple twenty gallon drums of water and – here is the fun part – it turned out they did have thermal protection suits. It was some kind of DARPA project and the suits were to be given to the army ... and to an obscure psychic research center in Cleveland.

I was starting to question my perception of how the world worked, because all this was even weirder than going on an expedition to Hell.

The suits were green long john type things, and had a kind of weird metallic sheen to them, which went oddly with what appeared to be knit wool. Perhaps it was harvested from electric sheep. They gave us a dozen of those in case we found some of the lost researchers. It still seemed excessive since surely we wouldn't find that many, but who knew how many bodies the researchers might have in Hell?

Meanwhile, to compensate for not giving us firearms, they gave us water guns for the holy water. They were those seriously crazy ones that only the most dedicated water gun fighters ever get: you could air-pressurize them, and carry additional water-ammunition in a back pack. Mine looked like a machine gun, only in purple. Emma's was green.

We put the suits on – they felt curiously neutral, neither hot nor cold – but not the backpacks, as they'd be cumbersome while sitting.

In the middle of the preparations, Emma asked if the priest had left, and when told he hadn't, she ran off with a box. She came back minutes later, and stowed the box in the car. Peeking in it, I saw it was full of water bottles. Since we already had a pallet of drinking water, I must have looked confused.

Emma grinned. "Those are blessed. They're not very good bottles, or very well sealed. If you drop them they explode. I know; I've used them before. The bottles, I mean. They're cheap. I used to buy that brand. But it got too messy."

"Oh?" I failed to see how cheap bottles were useful.

"Well, I figure we could throw them."

"Oh."

"All of it might disappear when you go through," the Jolie kept saying, in various ways, exasperated. "We're not even sure you'll go through, or whether the car will go through and you'll be left, suspended mid-air or something."

"I know," Emma said. "But that's no reason not to be prepared." Which made me want to laugh. I remembered her detail-oriented, gentle stubbornness well. It was part of the reason I loved her.

The thought surprised me. I realized yep, I still loved her, as much as I ever had. For all the good it was likely to do me.

Meanwhile I was trying to figure out more about this different environments thing.

"Well," Dr. Brant – who really kept insisting I call him Odd and was indeed odd – said, "the thing is that if Hell has any laws we haven't decoded them. We have decoded some for fairyland." He smiled at my surprise. "Yeah. It's a closer reality than Hell. Their laws sound very weird to us, like their inability to make raised bread, but there are reasons. For example non-sentients like yeast don't survive in what we'll call for lack of a better term fairyland. But that's about it. Also, the thing with iron seems to have to do with ionic resonance. It's not that iron hurts them as such, but it drags whatever parts of fairyland touch it into our reality, which often means they're burned or destroyed in fairyland, if that makes sense? Anyway, we don't know if there are laws in Hell, except the whim of those in charge.

"We have reason to believe – and no, I can't explain because it would take too long, other than to say we got two divergent but corroborating reports and … probes were also sent – that the visions of Hell, over the ages, by mystics and seers of various lands are accurate. But that doesn't mean that the visions would be the same for other people. The one thing that all humans seem to report is cold, sometimes a cold so intense that it's experienced as fire, and a sense of depression. But do understand you could find yourselves in a Chinese version of Hell, with flaying demons, and boiling caldrons of still-living humans. Well, now I think about it some of the medieval ideas of Hell in the West weren't that far different. So you might encounter that."

"I doubt it," I said. "We know who is in charge of Hell right now. And I doubt at six years of age she's learned much Chinese mythology or read a ton of medieval mystics."

"Yes," Dr. Brant said, dragging the word out, as though reluctant to admit it. "But the thing is, after you rescue her, she won't be in charge."

"If we rescue her," I said. And waved my hand, airily. "We'll burn that bridge when we come to it. And roast marshmallows on the fire. I hope Emma packed marshmallows. Now, how do we come back?"

"The charge we're putting on your vehicle is temporary," he said. "It should return naturally. And you should return if you are in it."

"And if we aren't?"

He made a gesture. And I made a note. Right. Try to stay in the Disgrace.

"How long will it last?"

He sighed. "Well, we can't be sure. Just … just do things as quickly as you can. Understand, I feel like I'm sending you on a no-return mission. I mean, if you survive, we'll know so much more. But I feel like your chances of survival are close to zero."

"It doesn't matter," I said, against my better judgment or perhaps against my worst judgment. "We're still going." And it made sense to me finally. I had to go.

Look, Emma was going to go. Rightly or wrongly, she viewed Lilly as hers to protect. I remembered Emma from elementary school. She always had a coterie of younger, more helpless kids she helped and took care of. I knew there was no point telling her not to go up against a bully when she was in this mood. Even if the bully was the big one. Arguably the biggest ever. And as for me? I'd go where Emma went. I'd once let her disappear from my life, convinced she could find better than me. But now, no real or imaginary dentist was going to get between me and the woman I loved. And I did love her. Once I'd realized that, there wasn't any room for waffling.

I didn't know how she felt about me. But I knew she had been lifting an unbearable burden without any help. Maybe she'd never have considered me as a romantic prospect, but if we'd stayed in touch, I could at least have helped her lift it. Instead I'd been cowed by dentists and rumors of dentists. And he'd never even existed. And I'd never even called her.

Well, I was done with that. No more dentists! Even if the "dentist" was Peggy in this case.

We got in the Brown Disgrace, finally, with me behind the wheel and Emma sharing the passenger side with a large tote full of yet more things that Emma thought we might remotely need, possibly including toothbrushes and almost for sure including healthy snacks.

The technicians, remarkably efficient for people called in in the middle of the night, had assembled a network of cables in the street in front of us. To either side of the street, they'd erected what looked like a forest of lightning rods. Cables dangled from the network, low eough to barely touch the top of the Disgrace, and they measured and calibrated their length precisely.

"There might be a flash as you go through," Dr. Brand said, leaning in the open window of the truck.

"How Back to the Future," I said, and he grinned, but didn't respond. Instead he looked towards Emma, "I'm hoping you do save some of our boys, too. One or more might even manage to get assigned to you as a psychopomps."

"A psycho what?" I asked, thinking that, of course, there would be psychos in Hell. I just hoped they wouldn't be dressed in someone else's skin and looking to eat us with fava beans and a nice chianti, but it was probably a vain hope.

"No, he means a guide," Emma said. "You know, like Laura to Dante."

Vague memories of 11th grade history floated up. "Oh. Yeah. Okay. So, someone dead who is in Hell will guide us?"

"Not necessarily someone dead or … someone who belongs in Hell," he said. "Could be … I do hope it is one of our boys, but well, it could also be someone earning his wings."

I nodded. That would be … interesting.

"Or we could be completely wrong," he said. "If you survive, you can tell us more." He smiled dazzlingly, as though willing himself to be certain. Then he stepped back and said, "You may put your window up."

If you survive.

I put the window up. Someone behind us slapped the Brown Disgrace's side, as if it were a nervous horse and shouted, "Go."

We went. I pushed the accelerator, while I reached my right hand, and Emma took it. She clasped it really, really hard. Her hand was soft and warm.

I shouted, "No dentists!"

Emma grinned at me. I'd told her at dinner that first evening that I thought she'd married a dentist. "Do you still think I had anything to do with a dentist? I never even dated a dentistry student!"

"Good," I said, approvingly. "Very good. I hear they have a talent to be inhumane. So, don't start now."

There was a bright flash, and then the Brown Disgrace was driving through Hell.

Which looked a lot like Cleveland. Or perhaps Detroit.

Except everything was on fire. And no one cared.

And that's when I noticed the guy in the back seat.

8 PSYCHOPOMPS

He didn't look terribly dead, except for being very pale. Looking around, I didn't see even a hint of sunshine, so the pale probably computed.

He grinned at me in the rearview mirror. "Good evening, Sir and Madam, my name is John Kincaid. I'll be your psychopomp for the evening," he said.

Well, he had one thing right. The psycho part. Though I'd never really thought of him as pompous.

"John!" I said. "I didn't know you worked for Infinite Mind." You see, I knew our guide. I hadn't seen him in about five years, but we'd been friends in high school.

"It was a temp job!" he said, sounding aggrieved. "I was laid off, and they offered great money, so I thought I could work for them while looking. I thought I'd be taking surveys at malls and stuff, to find out if anyone had a mind."

"Instead they sent you to Hell."

"Well, to be fair, lots of people had sent me to Hell before. I'd just never come here. I don't like it, Leb. Contains live bobcat. Wouldn't order again. It's a bad enough place to visit, but I was starting to think I'd have to live here."

Okay, maybe friends was stretching a point, as he'd been more geeky than I, which, yes, means he was very geeky indeed. He's been a member of the comic-book-and-science-fiction clique, and while I liked science fiction and comic books, I didn't have the patience required to spend hours arguing over the latest Spider-Man ret-con or debating the intricacies of JRR Tolkien versus JK Rowling. I liked that stuff, I didn't worship it. And I certainly didn't memorize it. Sure, both of us had spent our weekends playing RPG games, but he'd spent all summer doing it too. Which meant he was only slightly paler now than he'd been.

He wore a T-shirt and jeans, just as he had in high school, but this one failed to have a comic book character or a TV-SF-series character on it. Instead, it said in big letters, Wrong Fan Having Wrong Fun.

He laughed. "I wanted to wear a seersucker suit and a pith helmet, but they didn't let me.

Okay....

Above it, he certainly didn't look like one of the damned. I was getting an eyeful of those outside the window. They looked ... I think the only word possible was interesting, pronounced with a throat clearing, in a warning tone. One looked like a spikey pineapple stroking a penis in the shape of a spikey pineapple. Another looked like a hippopotamus-spider. And there was a thing climbing one of the buildings that looked exactly like Godzilla crossed with Cthulhu. But the scariest ones were the human ones.

There were people who said that they could see his eventual damnation in the eyes of the chief 9/11 hijacker. Imagine that sense of ... hatred for all living, that sense of lack of soul, but spread to an entire body. The despair, the hatred, the sheer coldness was there in the way they walked, the way they chased each other, the way they turned around to glare at the Brown Disgrace, the way one of them launched himself at our car, only for the Brown Disgrace to – gallantly – catch him cross-body with its dented corner, and somehow cause him to explode, bits of human-shaped demon flaring up mid-air like ... like an explosion of burning paper bits.

I turned my windshield wipers on. Don't ask, but they seemed to work to clear my view.

In the rearview mirror, I caught a glimpse of John Kincaid's cheerful face. His hairline had started receding. Nothing dramatic, mind you. But other than that, his cheerful, cheeky face, and the light brown hair were the same they'd been in high school.

His eyes sparkled at me. "You're going to ask what I'm in for."

"They said you just got lost in here," I said. I swear something that looked uncommonly like Bertie Schneider ran in front of my car, chasing someone or something with an upraised guitar. Bertie, the someone and the guitar were all on fire. His head flip flopped around, and even through the flames it was obvious that there was a hole in the place of his heart.

"Oh... er... heck, I was hoping to convince you I'd committed horrible crimes, all about being just a wrong fan having wrong fun."

"Some wrong fun it would have to be to land you here."

"Nah. I just got separated from the rest of the group. I've been wandering around for a while, and it gets to you. I was starting to feel the coldest despair when this guy called Azariah ... only I have an idea he's an angel, really, and can't tell you why–"

"Being an angel here wouldn't be a reassurance."

"No, but I think he's one of the good ones. I don't know what he's doing here, no. But anyway, he told me I should meet you, and ... well, he zapped

75

me into your back seat. I can't explain either. But he said I'd be given knowledge and that you're my second chance to get out of here."

"I see," I said. "And you're supposed to guide us."

"Sure." His grin was maniacal. "I'm your dread and terrible guide to these infernal regions."

"John, now, seriously," Emma said, and I remembered she was friendly with all the comic and SF geeks. Not just me. Mostly because she'd never met an underdog she could pass up on protecting and most SF geeks presented curiously unprotected. "Can you guide us?"

"Sure. I've been here … well, it feels like forever. And while it still makes no sense whatsoever, after a while you get sense for how things work. Also, Azariah said he'd put knowledge in my head. I assume you don't want to do all the circles thing and visit various people suffering torments, so that you can write a great and exemplary poetic work about it all to torture school children through the ages."

I dodged a demon shaped like a grizzly bear with tentacles who was trying to grab the Brown Disgrace. That meant I ran over three other demons, who looked like evil teddy bears with really large teeth. Under the big tires of the Brown Disgrace they felt like an unusually bumpy road.

There was fire everywhere, and for all I know the car was on fire too. Not that anyone would be able to tell. "John, cut the crap. Where is Lilly? The little girl who is here, bodily. Just take us to her as fast as possible."

"Oh. I thought you'd never ask," he said, "Take a right here. No, ignore the building. Just go into it."

Afraid that I was about to hear a loud "crunch" and smash, I turned, and drove towards a building that looked much like the one where Infinite Mind had its headquarters. And flinched from the inevitable crunch.

There was a sound like breaking glass as we first touched. But then the building exploded, and suddenly we were driving through a vast, arid plain. It was mostly treeless, and devoid of life. A lake shimmered in the distance, and the plain was filled, chockablock, with Roman legionnaires, and some other kind of ancient warriors.

There was blood and fighting everywhere. And as I hit them there was a lot more blood and screams. There was nowhere to drive that wasn't filled with people. I reminded myself they were all dead. Weren't going to get any deader.

The Brown Disgrace powered through the first dozen legionnaires, before the others screamed and started running away.

"Marvelous car, this," John said. "I have to get me one of these."

"There are probably a bunch of them in Hell," I said. "Do I continue straight on?"

"No, turn right here."

We did. And suddenly we were driving on the ceiling of a vast and empty amphitheater that appeared to be made of spun glass. From somewhere came a buzzing like a thousand angry mosquitos.

I don't know how dancing on the ceiling is, but do you know how hard it is to drive on the ceiling? Even if you know you're in a place where all physics is suspended, your mind doesn't really believe it, and you're fighting this feeling that any moment you're going to fall on the roof of your car.

Emma reached out and held my hand. It was a comfort. It felt real, where nothing else was.

"So, you guys are still together," John said. "I always used to be so jealous of how great you were together." Weirdly, even though he was one of the dead guys, he was looking down wildly and talking through clenched teeth and gave the impression that he was talking to distract himself so he wouldn't, you know, be scared of falling on his head.

"We were never together," Emma said. "I'm not Leb's type."

I looked towards her, surprised, "You're not my type? What the hell does that mean? Are you out—" and we started to fall.

John yelled. "No, no, no. Turn left. Turn left, Leb, now, and step on it."

What in hell could I do? Literally, I yanked the wheel hard left and stood on the gas. The Brown Disgrace had many issues, but none of those was lack of pickup. Though what the hell it found for the tires to push against when we were midair, mid-fall, with what looked like a forest of people on stakes beneath us, I don't know.

As I closed my eyes against the sight of the impaled people, who were still alive, grimacing and crying in eternal torment, the Brown Disgrace zoomed forward, turned itself right side up, and suddenly we were in an Alice-in-Wonderland landscape, filled with trees on which candy and ice cream cones grew. There were palm-sized pink butterflies everywhere.

In the middle of it, people were having a picnic. Well, one of them was a people.

I mean, there was a little girl, in a pinafore, accompanied by several demons about her size, also in pinafores. There was also a really large demon, with recurved horns and flashing eyes, and red pigtails with pink ribbons. The group was surrounded by teddy bears, and appeared to be having tea from a delightful-looking rose-painted Victorian tea set.

The little girl jumped up and waved at us.

9 TEDDY BEAR PICNIC … IN HELL

I HAVE NO IDEA HOW LILLY HAD SEEN EMMA, since we were all still in the Brown Disgrace, but suddenly she was running towards us, waving. "Emma, Emma, you came. Oh, I'm so glad you came."
She ran in front of the Disgrace, in a flurry of fluttering pink ruffles, and I stomped on the brakes. The side effect of being corporeal was that the Brown Disgrace could squish her. And she looked corporeal. Very.
Under normal conditions, the Disgrace stopped pretty well for a behemoth its size. But of course, these weren't exactly normal driving conditions. The green grass – if it was grass – under the tires squished and the car skated, so that I stopped just inches from Lilly.
In a way, a part of my brain was going, "She moves just as I'd expect from her picture and what I heard about her from everyone who knew her." And the other part was cringing and waiting for the impact.
I stopped inches from the little kid in frills, and she looked at the Brown Disgrace, surprised, her big green eyes wide open, as though wondering how it had got there. And then she came around to the passenger side, and John said, "Don't get out, don't get–"
But it was already too late, as Emma had opened the door and was tumbling out.
She dropped to her knees and hugged Lilly, "Oh, Lilly, sweetie, I thought we'd lost you. I thought you were gone."
Lilly pulled back, looking a little puzzled. She looked like kids do when they're afraid adults will demand the kids stop running around painting the walls with Kool-Aid and tying ribbons to the cat. "I'm fine." She grinned. She had two missing front teeth. "I've been having fun. There was this funny creature in my closet, and he said I could have fun and brought me here, and I've been having fun except I missed you, but when I went to your house and called you to come, you didn't." Her lower lip protruded. It trembled. I felt myself

turn to jelly. Apparently the lip thing was potent. I imagined what it did to Emma.

"Why didn't you come? Peggy said it was because you didn't love me, and you didn't want to come and play with me." She looked at the big demon with recurved horns, when she said Peggy.

Emma gave Peggy the hairy eyeball. Metaphorically. I guess in a place like this it could be literal but there were no real ocular organs handed over.

Peggy, by the way, looked ridiculous. Big, evil entities who towered above mere humans, had recurved horns, vaguely caprine features of indescribable dread, and off whom there rolled a sense of evil, like black, putrid-smelling oil, shouldn't dress in pinafores nor wear pigtails with pink bows. Nor did such adornments do a thing to make him look less evil.

I'm fairly sure all fashion advisors would agree. But the weird thing was that Lilly didn't seem even slightly scared. Almost like she wasn't seeing what we saw, which I guess might very well be true. That Father of Lies stuff and all.

Emma sighed. "That's not true. I do love you. I wanted to reach you more than anything. I just didn't want to come here without a way of going back, without a way of seeing you safe. We found a way as soon as we could and we came to get you."

Lilly took another step back. She looked up at Peggy and then at all the little demons, all dressed in Alice-in-Wonderland outfits. One of the demons was running his clawed foot in front of him and twisting the hem of his little pink gingham dress, exactly like a little, shy three year old. Despite looking like nothing so much as an evil hedgehog with recurved horns, it managed to look cute.

Lilly looked at them, then back at Emma, then back at Peggy all the while looking like a faun on the verge of bolting. "But I don't want to go," she said. "I've been having so much fun."

"You have to come," I said. "You can't survive here. Not for long. Not as you are."

"Oh, no," she said. "Emma why did you bring him?" She turned to look at me, and glared. "I know who you are. You're the man who tried to stop the nice music about kittens and puppies. I don't like you." She waved a hand. "Get him out of here."

The scene broke up. Demons in pinafores ran towards the driver's door. Let me tell you, they weren't even a little bit cute. They might look somewhat like very large hedgehogs with glowing red eyes, wearing pinafores, but it wasn't pretty when they opened their mouths to reveal row upon row of sharp, serrated, shiny steel teeth. They came at us in a pack, snarling like dogs.

"Leb, watch it!" came from John.

One of the demons had got into the passenger side, its teeth crunching so close to my arm I could feel a breeze as they closed. I punched it in the face, with an explosive sound, and Emma, who was still talking to Lilly, reached in, and grabbed it by the feet. I registered, in some surprise, that it had long chicken legs, ending in chicken feet with big steel claws. Emma grabbed it by the feet and flung it over her shoulder away from the car, seemingly without even looking. It made whoop whoop whoop sounds as it flew, and landed in a mushroom-shaped cloud of noxious-looking green smoke.

Emma closed the door. I couldn't hear what she was saying, and that was unacceptable, particularly as I saw Lilly start to pull Emma by the hand towards the picnic of the damned.

I fumbled for the handle of the door.

"I want to emphasize," John said, "that under no circumstances should you leave this car. It's your way back, and it could go back at any minute, leaving you stranded."

"No. I'm going out. You have to pick whether you're staying with us or the car."

"Leb, you can't be serious. We should go."

"What? And leave Emma stranded here? We're going wherever she goes."

"And then we'll all be stranded here," John said. "You have no idea what it's like. If you knew you wouldn't even consider it. We can more easily recover her from Earth."

"They couldn't even recover you. Besides where she is, there is paradise."

"Mark Twain is not sacred scripture. Neither are Eagles lyrics. Why are you guys here for some random kid? Why didn't you have kids of your own?"

"Because we aren't married."

"You really aren't? I thought you were joking."

"No. I never had the courage to even ask her to date. It doesn't matter. I'm never leaving her again." Outside my window, the demons were crawling, biting at the Brown Disgrace with their steel teeth. Their saliva etched the glass and from the sound, they were tearing out pieces of the body of the car. I'd guess that when you were in Hell corporeally, they could touch you without your consent. Fine. Whatever. I'd fight this out the only way I could. Of course that meant if I got out, they could touch me, not just my car. And none of it meant anything. If Emma was going to be stranded in Hell, so would I be. If she got torn to pieces, I'd get torn to pieces protecting her first. Because that's how this worked.

"Put on the prickly suit back there," I shouted at John, using my last shreds of sanity. "Like the one I'm wearing. And throw me that backpack with the super soaker."

There is a voice of command so absolute even John Kincaid will obey, I guess. He started to pull the suit on, and I crawled back over the seats grubbing in the back for the stainless steel baseball bats.

I grabbed one of them in two hands. I had seen Emma throw the demon, and I thought there was reason to believe a bat would work.

"Why the hell not?" John asked.

"Why the hell not what?"

"Why didn't you ever ask her out, much less marry her?"

Outside Emma was being dragged by Lilly and pushed by hedgehog demons towards the embroidered tablecloth with the china tea set on it.

What did a tea set do to end up in Hell? Was it used at a Satanic mass?

"Because there was a dentist," I said. "No, wait, there wasn't but someone told me there was. And I thought that would be so much better for Emma."

Emma tried to break away and cast an anguished look at me over her shoulder. Her mouth formed the word, "Go."

"John, zip that damn suit. Grab two of those filled backpacks in case the car vanishes, quickly. No, three. One for Emma. And a suit for her too."

My voice must still be working. I still expected he'd stay in the car in end, but he didn't say anything. When he reached for the wrong water bottles to move aside I said, "Grab some of those. Those are blessed. Emma wanted to use them to throw."

John grinned, a wicked grin, and threw the whole pack in a bag. "HolyHoly hand grenades of Antioch," he said, appreciatively.

We got the packs on. I took two them and John shouldered one and the bag. I guessed he was coming with me after all. We hefted the baseball bats like samurai swords.

I opened the door and hit a demon in the face, then shoved out. I heard John open his door and slide out.

I'd moved mom's medal from the pocket of my jeans to the breast pocket of my protective suit, and I swear I could feel it, warm, even though it was supposed to be impossible through the suit.

John yelled, "Oh, hell."

I had no idea why, and no time to look. A hedgehog demon came at me almost immediately. I hit it hard with the bat, and there were two more, one headed for my head. They seemed to fly, steel teeth chomping. Another was running along the ground, headed for my ankle. I only saw it by the corner of my eye, as I aimed at the flying one.

I heard a thunk, and then an echo of it, from my side. I hit the high one, then the low one. John seemed to be hitting them steadily too.

For a comics and sci-fi nerd, John sure could ply a baseball bat.

Yes, the demons made whoop whoop whoop sounds as they flew, followed by a cartoonish squeak and a kaboom as they hit. I hit three more of them, and then a horde headed for us, and there was no way out. They were going to kill us and eat us. And we'd probably respawn in Hell and be subjected to all kinds of torments, until I became like one of those desperate evil creatures running around chasing others.

The thought was worst of all.

10 WITHOUT DISGRACE

I WAS SURROUNDED ON ALL SIDES BY WEIRD DEMONS, and at the back of the throng I saw what looked like Bertie, grinning evilly at me, flaming guitar raised, trying to elbow his way nearer. What had I ever done to him? But then maybe he hated everyone.

"How much worse can this get?" I asked John. My arms were getting tired, and the crowd around us grew. They smelled, too. No one ever mentions the smell of demons, but it's a lot like stink bugs when you step on them, if stink bugs were human size. And in a crowd.

John was sweating. He grinned, and it was either a tired or an evil grin. "Don't ask, man. Just don't ask. Not until you experience the pineapple dicks."

"What?"

Before he could answer, Emma yelled, "Lilly, stop them attacking Leb."

Somehow through the din around me, the shrieking of demons, the loud pings coming from the Disgrace – I didn't have time to look and see what was happening – and the *thunk* and *whomp* of the bat doing its work, I heard Lilly say, "But he doesn't like puppies and kit–"

"No, stop it now." I recognized that tone of voice, and wondered where Emma had acquired it. If she was just imitating her mom's voice when she called us inside at the end of the afternoon, she was an excellent mimic.

The voice's harmonics were, "universal mom to universal brat," and it demanded instant obedience.

Lilly obeyed. Perhaps it was impossible to disobey that tone. The, "Stop, all of you," was sullen. It didn't matter. The demons stopped, one of them just inches from my eyebrow, mouth wide open, teeth gleaming.

Lilly still sounded sullen as she turned to Emma, "He doesn't like puppies and kittens. I want my friends to make him go away. Then you and I can have fun!"

Emma looked very sad and very tired. I saw her over the horde of demons – probably a hundred, crammed between us, as she knelt again to be on a level with Lilly. She reached for Lilly's hands. By the way, I want to point out that the grass was weird underfoot. It felt squishy and squirmy, like each blade of grass was a writing tentacle. I couldn't imagine kneeling on that, but Emma did. "Lilly," she said, very seriously, "There is no making him go away. If you tell your ... friends to make him go away, they'll kill him. And he'll come back. And they'll kill again. Besides I don't want him to die. I love him."

She did? Did she mean *love-love* or just *love*?

"Oh, you could have other friends," Lilly said. She smiled, a dazzling smile. "And you could have me as your friend, forever."

"I am your friend, honey, but I also want to be friends with Leb. And besides, don't you think it's too much to kill someone because he doesn't like kittens and puppies? And by the way, you're wrong. He loves kittens and puppies."

Lilly looked doubtful. She looked towards me, as though trying to evaluate my love of baby animals of fur at a look. "But he doesn't like the music!"

"He doesn't like much in the way of music," Emma said. "I mean, he sings and stuff, but he's not, you know, into music."

Lilly looked doubtful. "He doesn't like the dark stuff, with all the men in mascara, better?"

Emma who knew my tastes ran more to country, shook her head. "I don't think he cares much about it one way or another, hon. He was just trying to figure out why people were dying."

"People were dying?" Lilly looked genuinely shocked. "You mean…."
Her eyes were rounded. "They really died?" She looked around in a
panic. "I thought it was a game."

"No. It wasn't a game. These are bad creatures, honey. If you tell
them to stop someone talking, the … creatures you're commanding do it
the only way they know how. They make that someone die. In really
horrible ways."

Lilly looked surprised, then said in a little voice, "Oh. You mean I
might have … I won't do it again. I promise I won't do it again." There
were tears in her eyes.

"No," Emma, said, standing up. "Because you're coming back with
us."

Lilly turned around. "But I don't want to go," she said. "It's lonely
there. My parents don't want me. It's always boring, except when they
want me to behave. And then it's horrible. And Mom said I need to go
to a boarding school because I'm destru—destructive." Her little face
turned red, and there were tears in her eyes.

"Are you destructive?" I asked.

She quirked her mouth, and looked at me, then back at Emma.
"You're sure he likes puppies and kittens?"

"Positive," Emma said, calmly. Her smile warmed me all through.

I had the impression the demon frozen inches from my face had
moved. At the back of the crowd, Bertie, who'd never stopped, kept
trying to find a way through the mass of frozen-in-place demons.

Just in case, I stepped around them to get a better view of Lilly.
"Really bad idea," John Kincaid muttered, but he walked behind me,
holding a baseball bat. Two other guys joined him. I couldn't see their
faces, and they weren't important.

Emma was still holding Lilly's hands, and Lilly was staring at me. "I
love puppies and kittens," I said. "I never got to have any because my
parents died when I was young, and my foster parents didn't like
animals in the house. But I'd love to have a family: lots of kids and
puppies and kittens." I looked towards Emma, whose eyes seemed full
of water, shining and reflecting the weird light of the plains of Hell. Did
her lips form the word *Yes* or was it just my impression?

Lilly gave a deep sniff. "You see," she told Emma, "there was the funny animal in the closet. The one with shark teeth. He said my parents needed to love me better. I tried to get their attention. I went to Mom's closet and I cut up Mom's best dress," she said. "I just took scissors to it and cut and cut."

"Why?" Emma asked.

"So ... so she wouldn't go out. I thought if she stayed at home, she might find out she liked doing things with me, and she might figu–figure out that I was ... might spend time with me. Like in the movies and stuff."

The kid looked caught between guilty and wishful, and then all too old as she sighed and said, "It didn't work. I should have known it wouldn't work. Our family isn't like the movies at all. She just got all upset and yelled. And Dad said I'd have to go to a boarding school, and then I wouldn't see Emma again, and Mom said Emma was a bad influence–"

Emma was shaking her head. "Remember what we talked about? You shouldn't destroy other people's things. They're not yours."

"I know, but he said it would work."

"They lie to you, honey, they've been lying all along. Come home with us."

"I don't want to. It's just back to *them*, and they won't even let me come to your house, now. They'll send me away to the stupid boarding school."

"If you won't come then I won't go. I'll stay with you," Emma said. "It's going to get very bad, and we'll probably die, but I'll stay with you."

"Me, too," I said.

Lilly looked from one to the other of us.

"We need to go," John said, behind me. "We have to get out of here. You're going to lose your ride home."

The Disgrace pinged, loudly.

"Emma," I said.

Emma bit her lip, obviously worried. Then she said, "Lilly please come. If we stay, we're going to be killed and tortured forever. Our car is going to go and we need to be in it. If you won't come we'll stay, but we don't want to die. If you come with us, I promise I'll protect you from boarding school."

This seemed doubly stupid to me, both the bluff and the promise, but Emma seemed to be very sure, and the car was pinging loudly.

"Lilly?"

Lilly nodded, and reached for Emma's hand.

Which is when all hell broke loose. By starting to leave, I guess she relinquished her hold on the forces of Hell.

Peggy roared, tearing at his ribbons and bows, and growing ten times larger. He drooled green stuff and screamed, "Get them."

At least I think that's what he screamed, though it was hard to tell what words were there amid the growling.

I grabbed Lilly's other hand, while somehow passing a stainless steel baseball bat to Emma. Don't ask me how. I don't know. I mean, my right hand was still firmly holding onto the baseball bat I meant to keep. For the purposes of this account, you're free to assume I grew a third hand.

There were demons all over between us and the car. Emma and I hit them with our baseball bats, but they kept getting closer, and Lilly was crying, babbling something about how she would be good in the future.

The Disgrace pinged loudly and … vanished.

I said words that probably added to my karmic load, or whatever, and made it easier for Hell to get to me. John Kincaid screamed in frustration, sounding much like Peggy, and suddenly he had the Super Soaker in his hands, and was spraying water all around.

I hadn't been sure what holy water would do in Hell. Turned out it was … pyrotechnic. It was like fireworks. Okay, so it was like fireworks if fireworks started with a sudden lava-like eruption of fire, that turned all kinds of bizarre colors at the edges.

It also didn't smell like fireworks. Or at least like no kind of fireworks I'd ever smelled. It smelled exactly like roasting stink bugs. What was left behind, though, was a sort of gooey pink residue bubbling a little.

Emma got the idea before me, and had her Super Soaker out, spraying. The three of us stood in a group, back to back, with Lilly between us, while around us the pink gooeyness grew.

Even Bertie – I saw – flamed up, and ran around in circles, while he turned into what looked like a little bit of bubblegum when the holy water hit him.

Then there were steps that make the Earth tremble, and I turned to fire, and … nothing.

It was Peggy. Okay, fine, Satan, though I still thought it was funnier – even if not entirely justified – to go on calling him Peggy. Hey, he still had bits of pink pinafore clinging to his gross goat-like haunches, and there were pigtails around his ugly mug.

But there was nothing funny about his roar. It was something about defiling the halls of Hell, and he was bearing down on us at a clip.

Emma's gun had also played out, and she grabbed her baseball bat from the pink goo. Satan's hoof almost stepped on her, and she gave it a good whackwhack. It smoked and caught fire, but he didn't seem to notice.

He reached down and grabbed John Kincaid, who screamed. Satan took John up to his monstrous face, grabbed between thumb and forefinger, and opened his maw, like John was an olive, and looked particularly tasty.

John had stopped screaming and was fumbling. Then he screamed again. I have no idea what he said, but he'd had his hand on his duffel bag, and now brought it out with … something.

As he threw it into Satan's open mouth, I recognized a water bottle. One of those that had been blessed.

There was a moment when everything stood perfectly still. Like the moment between lighting the fuse and the sound of the explosion.

John Kincaid was still suspended above us, thirty feet up or so.

Satan started to roar. He dropped John, who kind of managed to grab onto one of Satan's hairy arms, and started grabbing his way down, one tuft of hair at a time.

Which would not be nearly so scary if something very weird weren't happening to the Prince of Darkness at the exact same time. To wit, he was cracking, like clay exposed to heat. Big cracks were opening in the ugly face, the hairy body. Fire glowed red in the cracks.

He screamed, an indescribable sound. Like all the grand pianos that had once been used to produce Satanic music all hitting the same high and insane key at once.

John hit the part where Satan's thigh curved out and slid-ran down that, looking much like he was trying to surf.

Which is when Satan exploded. Burning bits of demon blew up all over, and I tried to deflect some of it, while Emma hunched over Lilly, protecting her.

Yes, I did worry about what had happened to John, but that was a worry of short duration, as I heard him say, "Great, I have melted demon all over me," from somewhere behind me.

When I looked again, I heard another roar, and there was a dark cloud heading towards us. John had somehow retained the duffle. I loped over to him, and reached into it. I grabbed a water bottle by touch, and threw it at the cloud.

It made a *clunk*, and the cloud cleared, revealing the Disgrace.

The guy driving it was eerily familiar, another of the high school geeks from back when. His name was Seamus Curran. What are the chances of two guys named Seamus in the same school? I think part of the reason we'd never become friends was precisely because it would be too weird. Grinning like a gonzo goofball, another of the geeks, Dave R. Man, sat beside Seamus.

They opened the doors and scrambled into the back. I climbed into the driver's seat as Emma clawed up into the passenger seat. It seemed to me that I already couldn't feel the solidity of the car as I climbed in, but it was more firm once I was inside. I closed my door.

Emma kept her door open. Lilly rushed, half running, half throwing herself under Emma's arm, and crammed onto Emma's lap, just before Emma closed the door.

From behind me, someone who wasn't John Kincaid said, "Oh, shit."

I saw him in the rearview mirror, as I gunned the Disgrace. "Seamus Curran," he said. "You probably don't remember me. And what I meant is, she just stepped off the throne of Hell. Now he is in control again."

Behind us, the bulk of *Peggy* was reassembling and growing into something like a building-size cloud with red glowing eyes. There were pieces of pink gingham in the wind, and they burned like Hell's fires.

"Gun it, gun it, gun it," the third guy said. Dave Mann. "Azariah told us where to find you. He drove the car to us. He said to drive … to drive like hell and not to stop, no matter what. Straight on till dawn."

And I was gunning it. We were driving over demons, which massed in front of us, trying to stop us. There were demons behind us too, chasing us. A mass of them. I was almost sure Bertie was among them. I could see the profile of the burning guitar in my rearview mirror. It seemed unfair he had it in for me. What had I done? Fail to save him from this? Well, so had everyone else.

"I suppose you were also working for Infinite Mind because you were unemployed?"

"It was good temp work!" Dave Mann said. "It seemed like a good idea the time."

"Last time I take a job that takes me to Hell," Seamus Curran said.

The Brown Disgrace tried. Look, it really tried. But there were demons all in front, and they understood the true technique of the human … er … demon wave.

I hit them with the car, and they burned and shredded, and my windshield wipers were going full time, clearing bits of demon, and—

We stopped. The Brown Disgrace puttered and came to a standstill, and the motor died. There were demons all over, hideous faces and countenances pressing against the windows. And from behind us came gigantic steps. I mean, the sort of steps you'd expect to hear if the Empire State Building went for a walk.

John had been in the back of the Disgrace, amid all the things, and as he passed out water guns to the other two guys, I realized he had been filling the tanks. He also, solemnly, passed out the cheap bottles of blessed water. Then he started to open the door.

"Where are you going?" I asked.

"The roof," Seamus Curran said. "As soon as you can start this again, drive off."

"But you'll fall off."

"Nah, got belts," Dave Mann said.

And like that, they opened the doors as much as they'd go, hitting the demons blocking them in the face with holy water. The smell of melting demon was unbelievable.

Lilly was very pale. We were all very pale. I mean, the guys who'd been in Hell started that way, but we were still pretty white. Even Emma. Every freckle stood in relief on her face, as she hugged Lilly with her right arm, and reached her left hand for my right. We held hands, like school kids.

Around us, the winds of Hell howled. Demons were tearing chunks of the car, or at least it sounded like it, in a hideous noise of ripped metal. And above us, it sounded like the guys were scrambling to – belt? – themselves to the roof rack. Jets of holy water flew down as well as the occasional "holy water grenade."

The demons screamed and shrieked, and burned.

I tried to start the Disgrace. It coughed, almost caught and stopped.

"She dared defile the throne of Hell," something I suspected was the former *Peggy* said behind us. "Hand her over and I'll let you go."

Images of Bertie Schneider's eaten-out heart came to mind. We could hand her over, of course. But she was a little girl. And she'd been as innocent as it was possible to be in Hell. She'd had no idea what she was doing. She'd been raised by worse than bears.

"No," I shouted. And saw Lilly lift an astonished face from Emma's shoulder. Emma smiled at me and patted Lilly's back.

"If you don't leave her, you'll all be punished. None of you shall escape the fate of the damned."

Some of those faces pressing against the window looked like Escher's living nightmares.

This time, it was Emma who shouted, "Never. She's ours. You can never have her."

"Drive, Leb, damn it," John Kincaid shouted from the roof. He was concentrating the holy water fire in front, and most of the demons there were gone, save for burning piles of melted pink demon goo.

Which is when my brain started working. Emma was right, of course. It was all or nothing Either we all left, or we all stayed. There was no other way out. None. It was all for one, and one for all.

"Go!" someone screamed from atop the car, as a new wave of demons headed for us. I prayed the guys on top would hold fast, stomped on the gas twice to prime her, and turned the key. The

Disgrace turned over beautifully and with the guys on the roof throwing holy water in all directions, I pressed on the gas. And nothing happened. I realized we were being held in place by some kind of supernatural force. Behind, the demon formerly known as Peggy drew nearer.

Gnad's voice echoed in my mind, saying they couldn't touch us. Not without our consent. And "we" extended to the Disgrace.

"You have no power over us," I screamed. "No power. Let us go, in the name of the Most High." I stomped on the gas, and like the sun rising over a night of nightmares, like the first bird of spring, like the first note of an hallelujah chorus, the Brown Disgrace leapt forward.

The demons didn't vanish, but they exploded and burned as we drove through them.

Everything was on fire, Earth and sky alike. And everything was equally dark. With streaks of purple shining through the maelstrom.

Forward. And I wished this guy, Azariah, who might be an angel, might come to our aid.

Suddenly there was … a Roman centurion, helmet and all, with long blond hair and wings. He held a lance, and ran ahead of us. We could see him clearly even through the fire. And he had wings. And the wings were not black or on fire, so he probably was one of the good guys.

I followed. I certainly seemed in no danger of hitting him. For one, he was growing, until the Disgrace was about the size of his calligas. And he ran ahead of us though the burning plane.

Someone on the roof yelled, "Yippee Ki Yay, motherfucker" and a jet of water hit a largish pineapple-demon and made him explode. I think it was John.

The Disgrace hit a bump and seemed to hang weightless in the air for a moment.

Well ahead of us, the angel turned around and stepped aside. Without speaking, he indicated that we should drive around him. He pointed with his spear. Ahead of us there was a rosy glow like the sunrise, visible even through the burning. I gunned it toward the glow, and drove straight ahead.

Behind us, I was aware of some kind of battle. There was a weird wind around us, and the Disgrace was pinging continuously.

I expected at least a flash of lightning, but there was none. The burning just stopped. The air stopped smelling like burnt demon.

Suddenly we were just driving on the streets of Cleveland. There were guys on either side of the road, dressed in clean-suits, like the employees of Infinite Mind had been.

And the radio came on. It was the end of American Pie. *I saw Satan laughing with delight.*

I felt the blood drain from my face and turned to see Emma equally pale, clutching Lilly. But we were all here. We were all together.

Dr. Odd was running towards us. The guys were climbing down from the roof.

"Three," Dr. Odd said. "You found three of them!"

I must have got my car door open and stepped out, because the Doctor shook my hand, effusively. I was vaguely aware of Jolie helping Emma and Lilly out of the car.

John Kincaid slid down the side of the car. Seamus Curran punched me in the upper arm, in what I suppose was a sign of comradery. He said "Dude!"

I was so tired I could have fallen asleep standing up. And there was someone trying to take my report, as I blinked owlishly at him.

"Let him go, let him go," Dr. Oddell said. "We'll talk to our guys first. Mr. Magis, do you have a business card? I will call you in the morning. We have this problem with the Loch Ness Monster."

I blinked. But if you make a living as a PI, you have some instincts so ground-in that you'll probably respond even if you are, in fact, clinically dead. I reached in, past the thermic protective suit, and got my card, and put it in his hand.

I checked on John, Dave and Seamus. They all had maniacal grins on their faces and were talking to guys in clean suits.

Lilly and Emma were out of the car. I felt more lonely and beaten than I'd ever felt. And I was sure, and had reason to believe, from dim recollections of the myths I'd studied, that the kind of incursion I'd performed would not go unpunished.

Feeling like something as large and namelessly evil as Peggy was bearing down on me, I got in my car. Emma and Lilly were talking to

Jolie. They didn't even see me go. Didn't even wave.

I drove home to my ratty apartment complex, opened the door.

I think I took the special suit off. I remember the fear making me clutch the medal in my hand and whisper, "Now I lay me down to sleep—"

And then I was asleep, and walking again in the Hell landscape, but this time the legionnaire with wings was beside me. "I don't remember an angel called Azariah," I said.

He grinned, a surprisingly engaging, boyish grin from someone I instinctively felt should be a thing of dread and majesty. "The name is Raphael," he said.

"Oh. And what is a nice archangel like you doing in a place like this?"

"Ah. Mr. Magis, now. You should know that no place is written off from God's mercy for those who need it."

"Not even Hell?"

"Not even Hell."

"But there will be vengeance," I said. "I can feel it."

"Vengeance is beyond his power. Except perhaps in small details. But you have called on boundless mercy and infinite protection as well. For the rest, you have to pray and hope. Like all other children of Eve. And perhaps what evil thinks is the ultimate vengeance will … not be."

"What?" I asked, visions of dying in my sleep creeping through my mind.

"Let's say the adversary doesn't understand human bonds, human love or human family except as a punishment."

"What?"

11 IN THE COOL LIGHT OF MORN

AND I WOKE UP.

For a moment, staring at the ceiling, feeling the sheets under and over me, and some kind of light eiderdown on me, I thought that I had dreamed everything.

Except I hadn't dreamed everything. Because this wasn't my room. I was staring at smooth plaster with a prim Victorian floral plaster border, which my crappy seventies vintage apartment had never had.

And I wasn't laying on my mattress bought from a discount store. And I'd never in my life owned an eiderdown. In fact I wasn't sure what eiderdown meant. I just knew this was is.

My phone was ringing. I reached out from under the covers, instinctively, to the bedside table, for it, and put it to my ear with a, "Yeah."

"You did it, man," Rando's voice. "I don't know how you did it, but you did it. This morning I'm getting phone calls from all these guys saying they don't know what came over them, but they're going back to their old style. Yesterday, Hade's Whores tore out the pink crap on stage and gave an amazing rendition of Flaming Handbasket. Everyone is talking about it, and the recording rep in the audience was impressed. I'm going to be all right, man."

"Good," I said, my head aching, as I remembered everything. Had I really gone to Hell? "Good. I'll send you a bill."

"Is that Rando?"

There was a woman's voice from next to me. No, wait, there was Emma next to me.

She sat up, looking at me, an eyebrow raised. She had her hair down, and she wore an old nightgown, the sort you don't wear for an assignation. You know, not frayed or anything, just much washed. And I was about to say she didn't look like that sort of girl, but my eyes caught a picture on her bedside table. And it was Emma in a wedding gown. And the mug smiling next to her was me. Only we were about eighteen.

If this wasn't a dream … something had happened. And I remembered Raphael saying the … Adversary thought of human bonds and family as a punishment.

My heart pounding as though it would escape my chest, I swallowed hard. Rando was saying something in my ear, but I wasn't sure what. Something about a check, some amount that seemed ludicrous. Probably as much as his desk had cost or something.

I focused on Emma. My voice felt like it was strangled and weak, but I spoke nonetheless. "No dentists!" I said.

She gave me an answering smile. For a moment, in her eyes, I saw that she remembered. That the dual reality remained for both of us. But the lonely, desperate reality was already facing for me and maybe for her. She shook her head. "That will be pretty hard to do, hon. Lilly needs her braces removed at some point."

And like that it all came back, memories that I knew weren't true, but which were true nonetheless. The last ten years as they now were or had been or whatever. The past that had got me to this present. I remembered marrying Emma straight out of high school. She'd gone to college. I'd got my license. And then we'd moved back to look after her mom, and we'd had Lilly. Lilly was our daughter, a delightful redheaded imp, who looked like Emma had at her age. She was ours.

I was dimly aware someone would think of this as punishment, but I wanted to sing with joy.

"Hey, Leb, if fifteen thousand isn't enough, I can—" For some reason Rando sounded worried. Well, you know, he had no clue what I'd done, did he? Or maybe he did.

I remembered my life with Emma at the same time I remembered my lonely life, and thinking Emma had married a dentist. I think both were true in a way. Reality had been reset. But—

I sat up. We were in Emma's parents' house, in the master bedroom. I presumed her mom was in one of the more easily defensible rooms. The ones we could watch to make sure she didn't wander off in the night. I ran to the window and looked out. Her roses were growing, looked undisturbed. But Rando—

"Mom, Mom, Mom, Dad, Dad, Dad!" Lilly, in pink pajamas with kittens and puppies all over, came running into the room. She was ours, all ours. She even looked a little like a miniature Emma. "You promised we'd have pancakes and go to the zoo when Mrs. Flores comes to watch grandma."

And I suddenly realized that demons are peculiarly daft. Peggy thought he was avenging himself on us by getting us married and giving us Lilly. Think about it. Lilly had taken over his throne and ordered him around. He thought—

But Lilly was ours.

I remembered childhood incidents. How Lilly had set the living room carpet on fire while trying to light a candle. How she'd once watered the piano.

Demons would think that was punishment. Except it wasn't. Exasperating, annoying, endearing. In other words, a human child, growing up. Scary incidents at the time, became pure joy once overcome.

And suddenly I laughed. Yeah, we were going to be fine.

"Okay twenty thousand," Rando said. "I'll get the check in the mail."

"Sure, that's fine," I said. I realized we were actually okay, financially. Mostly because, you know, I could stay with my mother-in-law so that Emma could work part time as a consulting psychologist for the local youth rehabilitation center. And I did earn okay. And we didn't have housing expenses.

Emma kissed me quickly and said, "I'm going to get Lilly bathed. Mrs. Flores said she'd be here at ten. It will be fun to have a day for just the three of us."

"Very fun," I said.

Emma frowned a little, "I had—" She hesitated and searched my eyes. "I remember a past where we'd never married, and Lilly wasn't ours. I'm so glad it was just a bad dream." She winked at me, and she went out of the room.

I heard her run water, while Lilly chattered incessantly. "Mom, Mom, Mom."

We really should have another kid. Soon.

The phone rang, "Mr. Magis?"

"Yes?" I said.

"Dr. Oddell here. I wonder when you'll have time to give us a report. We'll pay you for it, of course. We also need someone of your … peculiar talents to take care of a case in Denver for us."

"Sure. I'm … very busy all day, but–" The new memory, overlaid on the old, told me that we had arrangements for this. A calendar on the wall over the dresser. Emma had her work marked out on it, by day, as well as the days Mrs. Flores could sit with my mother-in-law and Lilly. I frowned at it. "I can come tomorrow morning."

"Excellent. We'll make it worth your while."

I hung up, tossed the phone on the bed before anyone else could call me, and walked out of the room and down the hallway, past the bathroom where Lilly was completely wrapped in a – pink – towel and Emma was letting the water out.

I went to the garage. I couldn't wait to see what I drove in this wonderful new life.

But there, under the garage lights, sat the Brown Disgrace. It didn't look any worse for its trip to Hell.

And it didn't look any better. Stolid, dented, the gasoline-guzzler seemed to snigger at me. I was still stuck with it. I had a feeling this was one car I'd always have.

I heard Satan laughing with delight.

The day the pink music died.

DEEP PINK

ABOUT THE AUTHOR

Sarah A. Hoyt is a bestselling author, who has published over 100 short stories and over 30 novels in science fiction, fantasy, mystery and historical fiction. Her first novel, Ill Met by Moonlight was a Mythopoeic Award finalist. Her novel Darkship Thieves won the Promeutheus award in 2011. Her novel Uncharted – written with Kevin J. Anderson – won the Dragon Award for Alternate history in 2018.

Sarah A. Hoyt was born and raised in Portugal and lives in Colorado with her husband and a variable-number clowder of cats. When not writing, she can be found reading, hiking, refinishing furniture or hitting the nearby greasy spoon for souvlaki.

If you enjoyed this book, please check for the next in the Magis series!